BARGAIN WITH A BEAST

INTERSTELLAR BRIDES® PROGRAM: THE
BEASTS
BOOK 6

GRACE GOODWIN

GET A FREE BOOK!

JOIN MY MAILING LIST TO BE THE FIRST TO KNOW OF NEW RELEASES, FREE BOOKS, SPECIAL PRICES AND OTHER AUTHOR GIVEAWAYS.

http://freescifiromance.com

FIND YOUR INTERSTELLAR MATCH!

YOUR mate is out there. Take the test today and discover your perfect match. Are you ready for a sexy alien mate (or two)?

VOLUNTEER NOW!
interstellarbridesprogram.com

1

Kovo, Atlan Warlord, Planet Atlan, Prison Cell 4-D7, Death Row

Time to execution: 00:10:12:43

I glanced at the timer counting down how much longer I would live. The small, black box was built into the wall in every cell. Some Atlans didn't want to know how much time they had left.

I needed to know exactly how long I must hold on to my tenuous control.

Ten hours, twelve minutes, forty-three seconds.

Forty-two.

Forty-one.

The beast within screamed his rage at my choice. The excess of fury did nothing but affirm I was making the correct decision. I was out of time. *We* were out of time.

I sat as I had been for most of the last few days, unmoving. Uncaring. The guards came each day, forcing me to eat, bathe and change clothing. I did what they told me to do with no argument. The beast inside me pounded the inside of my body, tore at my will, fought to break free, but outside I remained calm, icy control frozen on my face.

He'd been fighting me for years. I wasn't going to be able to hold him back much longer.

Why could the ten hours not be ten minutes? I was so fucking tired of fighting. Battling my beast. The Hive. The Intelligence Core. Mating Fever. Hope. The last was the worst of them all. Three years in the Interstellar Brides Program matching system and nothing. I had finally bested the most powerful enemy I had ever faced. I had killed hope.

I had no mate. Mating Fever was coming for me. I made this choice now before I lost the ability to decide for myself.

If I had to die, I would die with honor. I would die helping someone else. I had no regrets.

Down the long, echoing corridors of the facility that doubled as both research hospital and prison, I heard visitors speaking quietly. My senses automatically flared out to process the threat. Two warlords. Three...females?

What the fuck were fragile females doing in this horrifying place? They must be terrified. The males who escorted them had no honor, bringing them here, exposing them to so many dangerous monsters more than capable of killing them all without thought or control.

"No honor." Frustration at their stupidity forced a grumble from my throat.

The grumble increased to a growl, the growl to a roar.

"They claim to be warlords." They would not hear me, but the words needed to be said. Fools. Incompetent. Disgraceful. The males did not deserve the company of a single female. But three? Were they *trying* to get the females killed?

Another loud grumble escaped me. I had not fought in the Hive war, served in the I.C. and made this sacrifice so fools could escort innocent females around inside a death trap.

I roared, hoped the males would hear me and at least take the females under their protection to a much safer location. This floor of the prison was reserved for the worst cases, beasts so out of control they would kill their own family members with zero recognition or remorse.

Not so with me. I was here for the severity of my crime, not because I couldn't control my beast.

My beast would stay safely locked away until I did not need to worry about him—or anything else—anymore. Until I was dead. If I had to slice my own throat to prevent his escape, I would. By the gods, I would die with honor.

A quick glance at the little black box made me sigh. Two minutes had passed.

The next ten hours were going to be both the last, and the *longest,* of my life.

I settled into position on my bed, lying on my back, hands linked over my stomach and stared at the soft tones of gray and green meant to be calming.

Right. Nothing about this place was the slightest bit calm. We were all waiting to die.

That wasn't calm, that was fucking depressing.

"Stop, Adrian! Do not!" The loud command echoed down the corridor outside my cell. I sat up and swung my legs over the edge of the mattress. Motionless, listening to the faint pitter patter of what had to be very small feet.

A female? Walking toward this end of the facility? What the fuck was she thinking?

"Baby girl? What are you doing? Get away from there." A concerned, very feminine voice called out.

Baby? A female infant was here as well? Was that why the sound of the feet was so faint? They allowed an infant to wander freely? What. The. Fuck?

I would report these idiots to the Atlan council before my execution. This could not be permitted. The males in these containment cells were deadly. Out of control.

I rubbed my eyes with thick fingers and bit back a sigh. Had Atlan honor changed so much in the time I had been away that they no longer protected not just their females, but their young as well?

"I can't." The quiet confessions snapped my head around and I stared out into the dimly lit corridor, expected to find it empty.

A small female stood before me, watching me through the transparent energy barrier. Her eyes were green and gold, framed by long, dark lashes. Hypnotic. Her arm was raised into position as if her hand hovered over the control panel that held me locked inside. She wore a traditional Atlan gown the color of pale cream, but she was far too small to be one of us. Her hair fell in waves around her shoulders in a vibrant shade that reminded me of both rubies and copper, depending on the light and shadow that fell upon her. Her round breasts and curved hips entranced me. Her lips glistened in invitation, as if she'd painted them with liquid sugar, just to temp me.

Our gazes locked. My cock rose to attention. My beast rumbled deep within, where I'd buried him weeks ago. My beast, the rage I'd battled so vehemently to control, swelled and filled my mind with lust for this female. Need. *Want.*

Mine.

No! I denied him. I had no choice. This could not be happening. Not now.

"Adrian? What's up? Talk to me." A third female voice called out, this one younger. Brittle sounding. Anxious. Perhaps frightened.

Adrian turned her body to face those speaking to her, leaving her delicate face in profile. Gods be damned, she was beautiful. The masochist in me wanted her attention focused on me. Only me.

Mine! The beast wasn't just aware , he was insistent.

Clawing at my thoughts, fighting to take control. To take *her.*

Yes. Claim. Fuck. Mine. Bastard was persistent.

No! My mind yelled back.

"I can't leave him here." My mate—no, not mine, *not mine*—the female spoke with a calm, clear voice that seemed to soothe my beast, at least for a moment. She wasn't leaving us.

"Who?" The other female asked. "Can't leave who?"

Adrian shrugged. She turned her head to look at me over her shoulder. I looked into her eyes and nearly fell forward from the bed. Sheer force of will kept me locked in place, safely away from her. From touching her. Kissing her.

My cock jumped in response to the images playing in my mind. If she were truly mine, I would lift that gown to her hips, press her to the wall and my beast would slide his cock deep. I would devour her, eat her sweet core until she shuddered and sobbed her release. Then do it again. And again.

Pre-cum leaked from the tip as my entire body shuddered. I didn't dare blink. Could not tear my gaze from her, not for the smallest fraction of time, afraid I would miss something. I didn't have time to savor her as a beast should. I must be greedy now. Take the smallest gesture or expression and stow it away.

She licked her lips and I nearly groaned.

"I don't know. I don't know who he is."

Kovo, my lady. I am Warlord Kovo and I am yours.

"Then what are you doing?" The elder female, whom I now assumed must be my mate's mother—since she'd referred to this fully developed, seductive female as *baby girl*—sounded closer. Much closer.

Adrian stepped forward, still holding my hungry stare, and rested her forehead against the energy field. She was not Atlan. She was too small to be anything but human. From Earth. How was this possible? How did a human female end up inside an Atlan research and containment facility?

She lifted her hand and pressed her palm flat, as if she wanted to touch me.

I nearly ripped my clothing from my body in invitation. Jaw clenched, I did not move.

"They can't kill him, Mom."

"Daughter, he is here because he has mating fever." This voice was deep. Factual.

Finally, a male who spoke sense. The Warlord spoke in a soothing voice I'd heard my father use many times with my mother when I was young. A voice meant to calm. "He is dangerous. Out of control. He's probably not even aware of where he is or what he is doing. Do not release him from that cell. He could kill you, try to kill all of us."

I thought, perhaps, I should roar for good measure, prove his point. Scare this small female. At the very least, trigger the protective instincts of the male who accompanied her.

Her eyes bored into mine with knowledge. Somehow,

she knew. She *knew* she was mine. How the fuck was that possible? The male always recognized and claimed the female. My beast was more than ready to accommodate that need. However, that would provide no answer to my question. How did she know? I had neither moved nor spoken since she'd appeared. I stared at her because I could not look away.

"No. No, he won't." Adrian shook her head slowly, rolling her forehead back and forth against the energy field, looking at the monster within, looking at me. "He's mine."

I didn't move, barely dared breathe as a large warlord stepped into view with two additional females and one Atlan doctor I recognized all too well.

The females were, indeed, all humans. Small. They all wore traditional Atlan gowns, the elder in a dark, metallic color that nearly matched both her, and my mate's, hair. Definitely her mother. She wore mating cuffs that matched that of the Atlan with her, a male renowned for his time in the war, and infamous for his battle to be free of one of the Nexus units.

Had I been on duty, I would have asked him for more details. Fuck that, for *every* detail. But fighting the Hive was no longer my mission. My final mission was here. Now. Nearly complete.

I could not have a mate.

The third female looked very similar of face to my Adrian, except her hair was a rich, dark brown. Same gold and green eyes. But she was not mine. Her body did not call out to me. Her attention did not freeze me in place as if I were the lock and she the key.

"You are not to open that cell. He is not here for mating fever. He is one of our most dangerous criminals." The doctor spoke with authority. I both hoped Adrian would listen to him and dreaded the same. Perhaps, if I asked nicely, they would allow me to simply look and admire my female for the next few hours. That would have to be enough.

"What did he do?" Adrian asked.

The doctor began to lay out my crimes. Kidnapping. Treason. Murder.

I listened without reaction or remorse. I heard all if this too many times to count.

Adrian gasped when the doctor provided a few too many gory details about the murder scene. She would discover who and what I was. Her attention would be drawn elsewhere...

"That is more than enough, doctor." The warlord interrupted. Had I been capable of movement, my shoulders would have slumped in relief. As it was, my female looked into my eyes. I could not look away.

"I don't believe it."

"My daughter, all the doctor has told you is true. Warlord Kovo has been found guilty by both civilian and Coalition investigation teams. We neither accuse nor punish warlords without incontrovertible evidence. In fact, Kovo is the first warlord in prison for a crime— rather than mating fever—in a very long time."

"More than thirty years," the doctor confirmed the warlord's warning.

"Shit." Adrian turned her face from me and my entire body reacted. I shook with the need to ram my body into that energy field to get to her. I needed her.

No.

"We need to get to the lab, ladies." The mother waved her hands in small circles as if she could move her daughters with the slightest of breezes.

Adrian sighed. "You go ahead. I want to stay here for a minute."

"I'll stay with you." The young female in a soft, yellow gown offered her arm to Adrian, who slid her hand through and wrapped the two together.

"No." The warlord denied them. I wanted to kill him and congratulate him for being the only sane one here.

"Fine." Adrian didn't look at me, not once, as they all walked away.

I glanced at the countdown.

00:10:01:33

Fuck. Ten minutes ago I was ready to die, to do what I could to help Helion and the I.C. team accomplish their goal before I succumbed to mating fever. I was close to losing control of the beast. Too close.

Now all I could think about—all my beast could think about—was Adrian, hot and wet, her pussy bare and open and mine. Filling her up. Running my fingers through her hair. Tasting her mouth. Her skin. Her core. Putting mating cuffs on her wrists and filling her from behind as my beast was freed. Telling her over and over again that she was mine. That I was hers. That I would die to protect her. To keep her. To care for her.

I would do none of those things. I would die in ten hours, one minute, and thirty-three seconds.

Angry, frustrated, alone, I paced my cell, no longer able to remain stoic. Calm.

Time passed. I did not look at the countdown again. Too slow. Agonizingly slow.

I slammed my fists into the wall and roared with rage. With regret. With fucking bad timing.

"So, it *was* you I heard." The sweet, feminine voice silenced me instantly.

Turning my head, I found my mate and her sister both staring at me, hands on their hips. Stances, identical. Adrian's expression? Determined.

The other female had more sense. She had the decency to be nervous, biting her lower lip. "I don't know about this, sis."

"They won't even realize where I am until tomorrow."

"I know. But you know how much I hate lying to them. What if they check on us when they get home?"

Adrian chuckled. "They won't. Mom can't keep her hands off him. They'll be too busy bumping uglies to worry about where I am."

Bumping uglies? Ugly what? And why would they bump?

"I'll worry."

"That's why you're going to be back here in exactly four hours and let me out."

Stephanie looked at me, inspected me from head to toe. I remained silent. "What about him?"

"I'll figure it out. After."

After?

Stephanie's head dropped backward so that her face looked up at the ceiling. She groaned. "God. And you were making fun of mom for being a horny wench. This is insane. You know that, right?"

"I know. I don't care. I'm calling in my twin card."

"Oh, I know. You told me. Why the hell do you think I'm down here again? And low blow by the way. I used my twin card for that stupid calculus test."

Twin card?

"Not my fault I saved mine for something juicy." Adrian gathered her sister to her, their heads identical in height as well as form. In fact, the twins were remarkably similar except for my mate's beautiful hair. "Look. I'm going in there. I know what I know. I can't explain it, okay? You have to trust me."

The brown-haired twin's voice was muffled in her sister's neck. "Okay. But if you die, I'm going to be really, really mad at you. Like, forever mad."

I'm going in there?

Adrian's words finally registered, and I moved forward to tower over them as much as I could with the energy barrier still between us.

"You will not enter this cell, my lady." I was furious that she would take such a chance. Still, I could not force a threatening tone from my throat, not while I spoke to her.

And *my lady?* What evil spirit possessed me to speak those two words?

Fuck. What was happening to me? I should shout. Rage. Scream. Act like an out-of-control beast ready to rend and tear and kill. I could do none of those things. My beast, it seemed, had as tight a leash on me as I did on him. He would not allow me to frighten her. Would not allow me to disrespect her. Upset her. Injure her in body, mind or spirit.

Gods be damned. What the fuck was I going to do now? I could never offer her my mating cuffs. I could not. I would be executed in a matter of hours.

I could offer her nothing.

With a low rumble, my beast disagreed, shoving erotic images into my already fracturing mind.

Adrian released her sister and turned to face me. This close she was even smaller than she had at first appeared. Yet her eyes blazed with defiance. "Stephanie?"

"You sure? Really, really, really sure?" Her sister moved toward the control panel.

"Do not," I ordered.

"Twin card. Playing it. Now." Adrian ignored me.

Stephanie sighed. The energy barrier dropped.

Adrian took three steps forward. Her scent washed over me. My beast growled. My cock throbbed in pain. My vision blurred. I ordered my limbs to move, to remove this female from my cell. The beast took control of every cell, every muscle of my body. The transformation moved through me. My muscles screamed as they exploded, grew larger. My bones elongated. My beast shoved me aside as if I were no more than a wisp of fog in his peripheral vision.

The energy barrier reappeared, locking her inside the cell.

With me.

With my beast.

2

Adrian Davis

*W*hat had I done?

When I'd stepped into this cell I'd known, logically, that I'd be dealing with a man—alien. A large one, to be sure. Handsome as hell. A genuine sex-on-a-stick hottie. Dark eyes that looked right through me and made me feel naked.

No. Made me want to *be* naked. With him.

"Hi. I'm Adrian."

His gaze narrowed. He didn't move. Not even to twitch. Or blink.

"Can you hear me?" I'd heard him roar earlier and everything inside me had imploded. Rational thinking? Gone. One moment I'd been paying attention to literally everything from the shine on the strange, smooth floor to the oddly shaped lights. The next? My nipples were hard, my core throbbed. I began to shake from pure, raw, lust. Need. Like I was the freaking alien. And that was before I saw how deliciously sexy he was in the flesh.

There was no hope for me now. None. I didn't understand what I was doing, would be unable to explain it to any rational person. But I couldn't stop myself. He was mine. Like my leg was mine. Or my hands. My memories. My name.

Mine. Part of me in a way that didn't make sense.

"He's gone into beast mode," Stephanie shout-whispered at me.

"I know." Holy shit, did I know. My pussy clenched and I swallowed past the dry lump in my throat. I didn't want to talk to my sister right now. I wanted...other things. "Privacy screen please."

"You better be right about this."

"I am." Didn't know how I knew, but I did. "Four hours. Don't forget." We had an agreement. She would help me get in here, leave me alone, and come back in four hours to see if I was still alive. Or dead.

I was hoping for alive and very satisfied. Maybe even unable to move from orgasm overload. That would be acceptable, too.

"As if." Stephanie lifted her hand to the control panel and the energy barrier turned a strange, swirling muddle of opalescent grays and blues, impossible to see through. I'd taken the time to ask one of the doctor's technicians about it while mom and Max were busy with

their tests and scans and what—in my opinion—
amounted to torture. Tour complete, our mother and
new Atlan stepdad Maxus, or just Max as I secretly
called him in my head, had ordered us to go home under
the watchful eye of a couple of his personal security
team members.

A few faked feminine problems *down there* that
required multiple trips to ask the doctor questions, and a
handful of lies later, Steph and I had convinced each of
the guards that we were leaving with the other one, and
that Max had given each of them the rest of the day off.
We'd pulled the classic sleepover scheme we used when
we wanted to go to an all-night party mom would never
have allowed us to attend. My sister and I, and all of our
friends were all staying the night at someone else's house,
which was really no one's house...also known as party
time.

Was being good at lying—we'd been fooling our
teachers and just about everyone else about who was
who since we were young enough to talk—a virtue? Probably not. But the talent sure did come in handy if you
wanted to get your hands on a beast. Not just any old
beast, either. My beast. *Mine.*

How the hell I knew that, I could neither understand
nor explain. Frankly, the strength of the impulse was
terrifying. One stupid roar and here I was locking myself
into a cell with an Atlan who was, by all accounts, a
trained killer. A murderer.

He took one step forward. Stopped. I stood my

ground. I'd started this and I intended to finish it. Too damn late to change my mind now.

Besides, now that I was closer, he smelled divine. All pine needles, black pepper and a hint of something else. Lemon? Or maybe that was just him.

Our stepdad was also an Atlan warlord, but he didn't smell like *this*. Thank god. I didn't want to be lusting after my mom's new mate. That was gross. Whereas this Atlan was...tempting.

The Atlan gown I wore didn't have traditional panties underneath like I wore at home. Instead, I was pretty much naked, covered by five or six layers of soft fabric that swirled around my feet when I walked. I'd felt naughty and pretty all at once. There were more than enough layers to ensure no one could see anything I didn't want them to see.

No panties? Regretted it now. My thighs were coated in wet expectation—no, demand—for some banging, up-against-the-wall, sex. With a total stranger.

"This is nuts."

When he remained silent, staring, I took a step toward him. "Cat got your tongue? You were all orders and grumbling a minute ago."

He did not appear to be amused by my question. All he did was glare. And stare. And get bigger...down there.

Hah! I made a rhyme. I was a poet. Wouldn't my high school language arts teacher be proud.

"You should not be here, female."

"Well, I am." Problem with places like this, I decided,

was that trying to break in would be literally impossible. Scanners. Monitors. Guards. Lots and lots of guards...on the outside. But once you were in? They trusted these energy field things way too much. Sure they had monitors and stuff, but unless someone raised a fuss, no one paid much attention to the Atlans in these cells. Everything was automated. Feeding them. Clothing them. Bathing them. All on a schedule. It seemed crazy to me that they didn't have extra guards on all these levels, all day, every day.

Then again, who the hell would ever be stupid enough to want to break *in* to one of these cells with a raging lunatic who happened to be more than eight feet tall and able to rip one in half as easily as I might tear the wings off a butterfly?

Me. That's who. Quiet. Studious. Serious. Logical, *me.*

I didn't know where Steph was going to hide for the next four hours. Didn't care. I truly didn't.

I had my own problems. Eight feet tall, grumpy, grumbling, massive cock pointing at me through those hospital pants like a spear, kind of problems.

Well, woman, you've made your bed. Time to sleep in it.

Or with it.

I giggled at my own dumb joke. Not a funny, ha-ha sort of giggle. More the hysterical, what the hell was I thinking, type.

"Leave," he ordered.

"No."

"Get. Out."

"Nope." How cute. He was down to basic, one or two word sentences. Beasts were so charming. I'd seen Max go basic, horny beast around my mom enough times to know that if this beast were truly raging and out of control, I would already be dead. If he wasn't mine, he wouldn't be holding himself back with such strength.

Besides, his cock was speaking for him. That was a fact. And it was saying, '*Take me for a ride, Adrian. It will be fun.*'

His breathing sped up and I couldn't help but stare at the heaving of his massive chest. Damn, did I want to get my hands all over that. Every part of him. I inspected him from shoulders to feet. Even in the plain prison clothes—hospital clothes—whatever—there was no hiding his ripped muscles, broad shoulders, trim waist and thick thighs. His hands were the size of dinner plates and I gulped at the thought of him fucking me with a couple of those fingers. I'd always had a thing for hands. They showed character. Strong. Scarred. Sexy. His were...*yum.*

None of which helped calm me down. Rather, my crazy-o-meter ratcheted up a notch.

"I command...."

So, that's how it was going to be? Hmmm. I didn't let him finish before asking, "Have you ever met an Earth girl?"

"No."

"We don't really do that." I walked toward him, more convinced than ever that I was safe in here with him. If he wanted to hurt me, he would have. Instead, he was fighting with everything he had to keep his hands off me.

I was not interested in helping him achieve that goal.

When I was close enough, I craned my neck and looked way—*way*—up into his face. "You're too tall to talk to up there. Can you come down here, please?"

I expected him to bend. Instead, he shifted. Shrank. He was a very large man again.

"Still too tall."

"Gods be damned, female." He grumbled, but he also dropped to one knee before me like a knight.

Eye to eye now, I couldn't look away. His smell made me drunk. Literally. I could barely think.

Who was I kidding? I hadn't had a single worthy thought in this skull since the moment I'd heard him roar and my body had taken over.

"I'm going to touch your face. Okay?"

When he remained silent I lifted my hands to his cheeks and held his face between them. His jaw was big. His lips...big. Everything was big. I wanted all of it.

"I know this is crazy, okay? I know. But you're mine. My mate. I can't explain it, I just know."

"That is impossible."

"All I know, Kovo, can I call you that?"

He gave me a barely perceptible dip of his chin in assent.

"All I know, Kovo, is that you're mine. I can't walk away. I can't leave you. I want you."

"I am to be executed in a matter of hours, my lady."

"I don't care."

"I have been judged guilty of treason and murder. You should not debase yourself by touching me."

"Did you do it?"

"To what do you refer?"

"Commit treason? Murder someone who didn't deserve it?" I was no saint. The neighborhood we grew up in back on Earth didn't allow for that kind of naïveté. There were people who needed to die. Evil people. I doubted it mattered much what planet one was from. Evil was evil. It was universal. Someone had to kill those creeps. I was okay with that.

I expected him to answer me with either a yes or a no. Instead, he turned his head slightly to the side and refused to meet my gaze.

My gut instinct told me he had done no such thing. "Why are you taking the fall for something you didn't do?"

"Silence." His head snapped back up and he glowered at me. "You will not say such things. I was judged. My sentence is death." He lifted one hand and pointed to a countdown timer up in the corner of his cell, near the ceiling. "That is how much time I have left, my lady. You need to leave."

"No." I already knew about those stupid timers. I was going to fight to get him out of here. Find out what happened. Get him a better lawyer, or whatever they had on Atlan. Didn't they have appeals? Mistrials? Did their law work that way? I had no idea.

Max would help me; I knew he would. He was rich. Mansions and servants and people nodding to him on the street, rich. My mom would help, as would Stephanie, and all of Max's guards and friends and Atlans he knew. But to convince anyone to help me, I had to have some right to fight on Kovo's behalf, to speak for him. I had to be his mate. He had to be mine. Mine, mine. Mating cuffs on my wrists, mine.

Thick cock buried deep inside me, mine.

Yes, please.

"I command you to leave, female. You must obey."

"Only if I'm your mate. And, to be perfectly honest, probably not even then." I placed my hands on his shoulders. "Do you have mating fever?"

"Of course."

"How long?"

"To what do you refer?"

"How long have you suffered from mating fever?"

He shuddered. "Years."

Years? No wonder he was so ready to die. Everything our stepfather told us about mating fever was terrible. Burning in the muscles. Fogged thinking. Irritability. Headaches. Cock aches—although Max had said something less crude, like *swollen, angry body parts.* Yep. I knew exactly what he was talking about, especially after his face turned red.

Mom had kissed him then and shoed us out of the room. My sister and I hadn't just left, we'd *bolted.* Still wasn't sure we made it out of there before they were—umm. Not going to think about that.

"How did you control your beast for so long?" I was shocked that he would hold on for that length of time. Max had also told us that the most dangerous part of mating fever was that no matter how uncomfortable it was for the male, it was much worse for the beast. The beast *needed* a mate or he would eventually turn into a raging maniac, a monster that would take over the Atlan's mind and become obsessed with killing. Anything. Everything. Striking out. Desperately trying to stop the pain in both mind and body.

"We have no mate. I made the only choice available."

"The choice to die?" Lost in that killing haze, there was no hope for the Atlan beasts. They were locked away in places like this, to be executed. If they weren't on Atlan, they were killed out in the field by their own friends. Sometimes by a family member. Brothers killing brothers. Fathers killing sons. Horrifying. "But you're still in control. There is still hope."

"No. We will die. We must." His voice held no guilt. His gaze was steady, honest. He hid nothing. I did not see shame at his horrible actions or an out of control, homicidal killer. I saw...humility. Discipline.

What was up with this Atlan?

I glanced at the damn clock again. I was wasting time trying to argue with him or convince him to tell me what had happened to him. The idea of Kovo dying in a few hours made me want to kill something, or someone. That was not happening. None of this was. I was in here with an alien I barely knew but couldn't stop wanting to have sex with. For a week. Straight. Maybe longer, if he was as yummy as he looked. I did not believe he was a criminal or a murderer. A traitor? No way. Just, no. He wasn't crazy. He wasn't out of control. He didn't look or act guilty. Or ashamed. Remorseful. Nothing.

Something did not add up.

I'd raced in here like a lunatic because I refused to give up hope.

If I didn't do something now, right now, I never would. Courage? Draining out of my body with every second I delayed.

Shit.

In one smooth motion, I grabbed my gown by the waist and pulled the entire thing off over my head. I was naked with a giant kneeling before me.

Naked.

"I am your mate, Kovo. You are mine."

He opened his mouth to protest, but I placed my finger over his lips to silence him.

"I don't care how long we have."

Lie.

"If I can only have you for a few hours, then I'm going to make them count. I want to touch you. I want you to touch me. I want to kiss you, and I want your cock inside me."

Truth.

I leaned forward, every muscle in my body trembling

with nerves. I was going to kiss him. These warlords were lusty bastards, weren't they? I was naked, here. He was trying to be honorable, hadn't touched me yet.

Was I going to allow him to get away with that?

No freaking way.

I moved slowly, afraid I would startle him. Which seemed nonsensical. Me, startling a beast. But I knew he was holding on by a thread and I intended to break it.

Lips soft, I claimed his mouth, hands resting on his shoulders once more. I touched nothing else. His hands remained at his sides, but I stole a peek and found them to be in fists. Knuckles white. His neck muscles snapped into thick strands as if he were being attacked.

With a sound of pain, he tore his mouth away and turned his head to the side, to escape me.

I tried not to let it bother me, but I'd never exactly taken off all my clothes and literally begged a man to have sex with me before. Being rejected like this hurt. Made me feel stupid. I had been so sure if I could get close, tempt him, he would be unable to resist.

Guess the joke was on me. He'd fought mating fever for '*years*'. I was not sexy enough to—

"Mine!" The word was not spoken, it was bellowed by a deep, deep voice I'd never heard before.

One large hand wrapped around my waist, the other circled one thigh as Kovo lifted me off my feet and moved until my back was against the wall. He held me there and transformed, or completed his transformation into his beast. Jaw grew wider. Shoulders broader. Muscles seemed to swell up and make more muscles, and more. He got taller, too. Every single part of him grew. But it was the eyes that made my heart skip a beat, resume, then pound so hard I thought my ribs might bust open.

Facing me was not a calm and collected man. This was a raging beast and I'd thrown him the proverbial bone.

Me.

3

The Beast...

F uuuck, she was soft. I'd never felt anything that could match the softness of her thighs in my hands. The sweet smell of her wet pussy brought a growl to my throat. I could still taste her on my lips. Hungered for more. Fuck that. *Needed* more.

Not Kovo. Not that fool. Me. The beast who fought and killed for him. Who kept him safe. I kept them *all* safe and what did I receive for my honor? My years of service?

Torture. Torment. Dismissal. Betrayal by my own shared mind, by Kovo, the warlord.

I was nothing but a weapon, a deadly fucking weapon, but still nothing but a killer. Until her. My mate.

"Mine." My voice rumbled through her small frame. I felt the vibrations of the word in her very flesh.

I wanted to feel that again. Mark her. Take her. Fuck her. Fill her. Claim her.

"Mine. Mate."

Adrian. I'd heard her speak her name. I'd processed her scent and her voice. I knew she was mine, but the idiot, Kovo, would not listen. He had made the choice for both of us, the choice to be here, to accept punishment. To die.

Before her, I would have allowed Kovo's plan to proceed. I'd given up fighting it.

Now? I needed. My skin touching hers. My cock deep in her wet pussy. Her taste in my mouth. I was going to fuck her with my mouth, my fingers, my cock. I was going to take her and taste her and make her smell of my claim, fill her with my seed, make her come over and over again, her pussy wringing my cock with every pulse of pleasure.

She'd done what he had not been able to for years. Spring the lock I kept on his wrath, his fury. His pain. She let him *out*. Not just out, *out of control.*

"Skin." I needed to feel her breasts crushed to my bare chest. Her thighs wrapped around my hips.

Holding her in place with one arm under her luscious, round ass, I ripped the seams of my shirt with the other. Pulled until the fabric tore free and dropped it into a heap at my feet. My pants followed, my mate's eyes growing rounder, darker with each movement.

Naked as she, I pressed my body to hers. Breast to

chest. She lifted her legs and wrapped them around my hips. The head of my cock brushed the wet heat of her pussy.

I wanted to thrust hard. Deep. Take and take and take.

But she was so small. So fragile. I could not hurt her. Would not.

She lifted her chin and gazed up at me, looked me in the eye. "Why did you stop?"

"Hurt you."

"Oh." Her delicate face turned pink in a rosy blush. "I —uh—I'm not a virgin, but I don't have a lot of experience. I only had two real boyfriends, and they—"

Lowering my lips to hers, I stopped her with a kiss. I did not want to know anything about other males touching her. I heard what was important. She was not ready for what I wanted to do to her body.

Locked away, Kovo reminded me that we only had four hours. Less now. He yelled inside my mind, told me to let her go. Walk away. Follow our orders.

Silence!

With a red wall of fury, I blocked Kovo's voice, his arguments. I had listened long enough. I was in charge now.

Adrian whimpered and I realized I had kissed her too hard. I pulled back, but she followed. Wrapped her arms around my neck and held on in a near frenzy. Kissed *me*.

Kovo faded to a distant background noise in my head and I focused on my mate. Tongue in her sweet mouth, I mimicked what I would do to her with my cock. My hands massaged the full roundness of her ass. I brushed her pussy with my fingertips over and over until she was panting. Moaning. When she tried to force her way onto my cock, I lifted her higher, her back braced on my forearms, her pussy in mid-air and on display, her knees over my elbows so I could hold her open.

So I could feast.

I had no mercy in me, not when it came to her pleasure. I took her into my mouth, plunged my tongue deep into her wet heat. Pulled back and sucked her clit into my mouth. Over and over until her hands pulled at my hair and she strained to push her swollen flesh toward me. Into my mouth.

I allowed her shoulders to press back against the wall as I straightened my arms. Her ass rose toward the ceiling, her pussy rising to my lips.

It wasn't enough. More. I wanted more.

I shifted, holding the back of her neck in one hand, her body fully reclined on one arm I had braced against the wall.

This. Yes. Fuck her with my fingers as I sucked her clit. Open her up. Stretch her pussy so she was ready for me. All of me.

I worked one finger inside her and locked my lips over her swollen nub. I created a suction with my mouth, drawing that sensitive flesh inside my mouth and releasing it. Again. And again. Faster.

Her hands were frantic, grabbing my head. Tugging. Shaking. Letting go to start all over again.

I worked a second finger deep. She moaned.

My third finger made her pant. I bent them each in turn, looking for any sensitive spots inside her.

"Ahhh!"

If my mouth hadn't been full of pussy I would have smiled in victory. Found it.

I fucked her faster, rubbing my fingertip over the sensitive flesh I'd found inside. My tongue worked her clit, sucking and licking, judging her reactions and repeating the things that made her muscles go tight, her head tilt back. Made her hold her breathe.

She cried out, the sound nothing that resembled any language. The cry of a treasured female. Her pussy spasmed around my fingers as her orgasm took her from me for long seconds. Brought her back. She was still mine. My mouth tasted of her. Her wet heat was on my fingers, my lips, the tip of my aching cock.

I wiggled one finger. She moaned. I worked her again, right to the edge.

"What? What are you doing?" She gasped the question, not understanding until I lowered her into place over my cock.

"Fuck you now. Mine."

"Yes."

I slipped inside. *Fuuuck.* Her pussy was swollen inside. Tight as a hot fist. My cock ached with both agony and bliss.

So long. I'd waited so long, Trapped inside Kovo. No fucking. No females. No mate.

No hope.

I pressed her back to the wall once more and used my hands to pull the lobes of her bottom a bit to either side, stretched her open. Exposed her pussy.

She slipped down a bit more, took more of my cock. We both made a noise I didn't try to decipher. The warlord, the killer, the battle analyst had been pushed aside until only *this* remained.

Skin. Wet heat surrounding my cock. My mate's arms around my shoulders, her fingers digging into my muscle in a pointless effort to force me to move faster. Allow her to move. To take all of me.

Not. Yet. She had not begged. Said my name. She attempted to direct me when she should submit to me, to my touch. No other would ever give her pleasure like this. Kill to protect her. Care for her. She. Was. Mine.

Where were my mating cuffs? I would see them on her wrists, proudly wear my own. I was her beast and hers alone. Kovo could rot in the back of my mind, locked away and forsaken, as he had kept me. He chose to kill both of us. He did not deserve her. She would wear my mating cuffs. I would remain at her side.

"Kovo?" She wiggled her hips, tried to take more of me. I held her in place, my cock half in, half out of her body.

"Not Kovo."

She moaned and scratched my upper arms. "Beast."

As much as I did not wish to look away from her, I needed my mating cuffs. I would not fill her with my seed until she wore them. Until she was completely mine.

Until Kovo could not undo what I had done.

Every cell here had a pair of mating cuffs available, just in case. This one was no exception. I spotted them where Kovo had thrown them in a corner.

Holding Adrian carefully in place, I carried her to the corner. When I bent over to pick them up, her torso moved with mine, her long hair dangling down to sweep the floor. Her stomach arched. Her nipples pointed to the ceiling in blatant offering.

I tensed. Ached. Needed.

My cock slid deeper.

She released me and lifted her arms above her head to gain purchase on the wall. Using what leverage she had, she pushed her body closer. Her pussy slipped down over my cock. She whimpered. My cock jumped in response.

Fuck. I wasn't going to last long.

I grabbed the cuffs with my free hand and looked around, desperate for a way to open them without leaving her body. I did not want to leave her heat. Her slick pussy. I wanted the cuffs to be on my wrists so I could reach out and play with those hard nipples. Run my hand over her soft skin. Tease her clit with my fingertip as I filled her with my hard length.

"Hurry."

I glanced from her breasts to her face. She was watching me. I held up the cuffs and she lunged forward to grab them. The clenching of her abdomen as she rose, her inner muscles, clamped down on my cock like a merciless fist. I groaned.

"Give them to me."

She took them and settled them over her soft belly. Harsh breathing accompanied her fumbling with the fastenings. She figured them out quickly and I held out one hand. She clasped the cuff around my wrist. I placed that arm beneath her to hold her up and held out my bare arm. She snapped the second cuff around my arm and I pulled her hips close, thrust into her body. Deep. As deep inside her as I could get.

"I can't—" She moved her hips slightly, grinding against me with a primitive passion that made me choke down a growl. I didn't want to frighten her. Not now. Not when I was so close to having what I wanted. My cuffs on her wrists.

A mate. Mine. Forever.

Or at least as long as I—Kovo—lived.

"I can't focus when you--."

I tilted my hips and she moaned.

"Damn it. Just hold still."

I grinned but acquiesced. I was not sure I had ever grinned like this before. Prior to her, I had only ever smiled in anticipation of battle. Of killing.

Fucking my mate was far superior to killing the Hive.

She snapped a plain mating cuff on one delicate wrist, then the other. I would replace them with properly ornate, ancestral cuffs once I got out of here.

For now, they would suffice. A shot of pain, like the arrival of a burning ember, circled both wrists the moment the connection between our mating cuffs was made. I'd been waiting for that flash of fire for years. My mind knew what the weight on my wrists meant. My instincts tuned to her, only to her. Her smell. Her touch. Her breath. I knew where every strand of hair fell, where her fingers rested. I knew when her toes curled. I listened to her heart beating. Awareness flooded with every gasp, every blink of her eyelids. I became a lens focused solely on her.

My cock recognized the primal mark of a mate around my wrists, the weight and devotion to the female who claimed me part of my DNA. The hard length burned from the inside out, the sensation nearly bringing me to my knees.

How had warlords survived this sweet agony for centuries? Eons? This female had no idea the power she wielded. My loyalty was absolute. I was her beast. Her mate. A deadly weapon only she would now wield.

Buried balls deep, I became the beast they named me.

Instincts older than time screamed within me as I fucked her hard. Fast. Deep. I needed to hear her cry out in pleasure even more than I needed to come.

Backing her to the wall once more, I held her wrists over her head with one hand and slipped the other low, behind her, to slide around her ass. I pumped into her body like a machine as I played with her ass and the sensitive, stretched softness behind her wet pussy.

I discovered the way she liked to be rubbed. Teased. Both that soft flesh and her tight, virgin ass. I slipped the tip of a finger inside. Stroked her. Stretched her open just enough to make her frantic. I fucked her pussy in a hard rhythm. Faster.

She sobbed. Bit her lower lip. Her head thrashed from side to side, and I watched the play of light in her dark, red hair as her core pulsed around my cock in frenzied waves.

There was no mercy in me. None. I fucked her faster, stretched one orgasm to two. I played with her until she was a panting, sweaty, sexy mess.

Only then did I allow the fire to consume me. Cum exploded from my cock with such force I moaned in pleasure-pain. My balls tightened, consumed by their unique brand of agony as they pumped precious seed into my female.

If this was dying, I would do it a thousand times. Follow my mate to the other side of the galaxy. Do anything, kill anyone to protect her.

To keep her.

When we both stopped moving, I fought to regain control before Kovo could sneak into my mind and take over, force me to change. I was a beast, not a fool. The warlords, like Kovo, those who controlled a beast inside their minds, knew the danger they carried within. The intelligence. The power. The battle rage.

The obsession with a chosen female.

Not willing to leave her body, I pulled her to my chest and walked to the edge of my bed. There, I sat, Adrian in my lap, her head pressed to my chest, her knees on either side of my thighs and my cock still inside her.

"Mine." I wanted there to be no doubt.

"Totally." She melted into my embrace and seemed content to remain in my arms. Trusting. Sated. This pleased me greatly, a bizarre warmth spreading through my chest and up my neck. From there it dove deep, moved toward my spine, and reemerged behind my eyes. A strange, heavy pain that made my face ache and my heart hurt.

Despite these abnormal physical reactions, her one-word response forced another smile from me, the feeling entirely unnatural. My mate amused me. Seduced me. Owned me. I was not like males of other worlds. I did not have a choice. This female would be held above all others. Cherished. Worshipped. Protected. Pleasured. Only her happiness mattered to me now. Not war. Duty. Honor.

Fuck that. I'd served. I'd fought and killed and been betrayed. Left to die.

Sacrificed by the male who, even now, screamed and raged inside my mind, fought to be free.

Fuck him, too.

Inspecting the cell we occupied with new interest, I stroked my mate's back as gently as I could while looking for any signs of weakness. A gap. A crack in the wall. Anything.

I was not dying in this cage. I would take my mate and get the fuck out of here.

I didn't care who I had to kill to do it.

4

Adrian

I expected Kovo to be back to normal size when I opened my eyes.

Instead, I met the stare of a beast who appeared to have nothing else to look at but me. He cradled me to him like I was precious. Delicate. His hand traced a soothing pattern up and down my spine with a touch I'd never imagined could be so gentle. I was sore in the more delicate areas. Empty.

We were both still naked. I squirmed, just a bit, and something hard and long said hello in a very intimate way. I remembered exactly how long and hard and thick he was. How good it felt to have him buried deep inside me.

My pulse raced almost as quickly as my thoughts.

Whoa. Better slow down the hormones or Stefani would show up and find me in a very unladylike position.

Who cared? She'd probably be jealous. I had a beast to pet and she did not.

Just to prove that I could, I lifted my hand to his chest and ran my palm lightly up and down over his huge muscles. "How long was I out?"

My beast shrugged as if it made no difference to him.

He was schedule to be executed in a few hours and he wasn't paying attention to the time? What?

How I had managed to fall asleep, I had no idea. Then again, I'd had more orgasms with him than I'd had my entire life—at least with someone else in the room. Then there was the transport to Atlan, which was no picnic. The constant *talking*, and eating, and *talking*, and meeting people. Meeting *more* people.

Thank god for the NPU, universal translator thing they'd attached to my skull before transport. Headache had been a bitch, but I would have been completely helpless here without it. Overwhelmed and lost.

Turned out Max, our mother's new Atlan mate, was top tier famous. Not just *world* famous on Atlan. He was famous in the entire Coalition of Planets. Over two-hundred worlds with billions and billions of people. Aliens. People. Thinking about that many aliens would make my brain explode.

Worse, Stefani and I had discovered that, apparently, human women had become somewhat notorious in the entire Coalition as well. For what, I still wasn't quite sure.

No one would give me a straight answer when I asked. Mom was no help, she just laughed.

Warlord Maxus, infamous Hive survivor and all-around badass warlord with a new human mate *and* two human daughters?

Our quiet visit to our mother's new home planet had become an oversized circus.

Entirely too many visitors to mom and Max's new estate. Mansion. Stefani and I were expected to get dressed up like the Atlan women and be social. Make a good impression. Represent Earth well so these people didn't think we were nothing more than a bunch of impolite barbarians.

I had news for my mother. We were exactly that. But I hated disappointing my mother, so I put on the dresses and talked and smiled and generally made myself miserable.

I was going to need a vacation from this vacation. Like two weeks locked in my bedroom, alone, to try to recoup everything I'd lost to the energy vampires constantly talking to me. There was a big gathering tonight, matter of fact. World leaders and shit like that coming to Max's house to peek at the circus freaks, the identical twins from Earth.

God. Even the thought made me shudder. Introvert 101? I could teach that class with my eyes closed, my mouth taped shut and both hands behind my back so I didn't have to *hug* anyone.

"No."

Startled back to the present, I looked up at my beast. "No, what?"

"No stop." He looked at my hand where it lay still and forgotten on his chest. I laughed.

"You don't want me to stop petting you, huh?"

"No stop."

Man—alien—of few words. This basic form of communication was growing on me.

As requested, I resumed stroking his warm chest, but dared a peek at the clock. Three hours had passed. I had one hour left to figure out what to do next. Step one, have sex with the beast and get his mating cuffs on my wrists? Complete.

Step two?

I hadn't worked all the kinks out of that one yet. I had thought to leave with my sister when she arrived, get ready for tonight's event and plead Kovo's case to the Atlan council members who would be at Max's house. They were the elected leaders of the whole planet, right? Surely one of them could grant a pardon, or at least a stay of execution to buy us some time.

I didn't know *exactly* what Kovo was accused of. Frankly, I didn't care. Scary, but true. I firmly believed that if he'd killed someone, they must have needed killing. Facts were facts. Someone had to take out the bad guys. Besides, Kovo had a mate now—me—so no more possibility of a crazed, homicidal beast tearing down the walls because he was so consumed with mating fever.

I needed details. I needed Maxus, my rich, famous,

Atlan stepfather to get involved. I needed help. This wasn't my world. I had no idea how things like trials and juries and police investigations worked. I had no idea what Kovo's rights were, or mine.

Based on the way he was staring at me, holding me, petting me—he wasn't going to be too happy when I told him I had to leave him here to go take care of some business.

"Kovo?"

"No."

Oh, yeah. He didn't want me to call him that when he was like this. "Beast?"

"Mate."

I took a deep breath. "That clock in the corner has less than seven hours left."

He did not respond. Great.

"I, uh, I am going to have to go home when my sister arrives."

"No. Mine. Stay." The hand stroking my back remained gentle, but the arm he had wrapped around my body tightened, pulling me closer.

Oh, shit. This beast was not going to allow me to walk out of here. I'd *assumed* that after the sexy times, the man side of him would come back out. I could talk to *him*. Reason with him. Explain that I wanted to help and maybe even get some ideas from him about how to proceed. Some help with the plan I didn't really have.

Was my sister coming soon? Was she okay? I hoped she hadn't been caught. What was I going to do if she didn't come back at all? What if she was in a stupid jail cell somewhere? Or in an interrogation room refusing to tell them where I was? What if some beast had decided she was *his* mate and she had her back against another wall, somewhere else, with a huge beast's cock pounding her into bliss? Talk about bad timing.

"No stop."

I blinked and realized my thoughts had wandered away from here. Again. "Sorry." I petted him some more. Trying to think and touch him at the same time was basically impossible.

"Aren't you going to shift back to your regular size?"

He snorted as if I'd insulted him. "No. This my size."

"You aren't going to change back?"

"No."

"Ever?"

"No."

What was I missing here? This wasn't normal, was it? Wasn't the beast supposed to appear for battle, claiming his mate, and...what? I couldn't think of anything else I'd heard of or read about. Beast comes out, claims his woman, slaps mating cuffs on her and bam. Done. He goes back inside and the regular version of an oversized Atlan male returns. Right?

How was I going to talk enough sense into this beast to get out of here? He would not hurt me. I wasn't worried about that. But how was I going to help him if he was too stubborn to let me go? This had disaster written all over it.

"Change back. I need to talk to Kovo."

"No. Talk. Now."

He truly had no intention of changing back into the manly version of himself. Had this ever even happened before? Didn't the beast have to change back? Wasn't that just how it worked?

I took a deep breath to try to calm down. Big mistake. Huge.

His smell made me feel drunk. Literally. Dizzy. Unable to focus. Aroused. The warmth of his chest beneath my cheek was no help. All I had to do to taste him was turn my head a little and press my lips to his skin.

My obsession was even worse than before I'd had sex with him. Which, if you'd asked me a few hours ago, I would have declared impossible.

Unable to resist, I placed a kiss on his skin and breathed him in for a count of three. His cock twitched.

I scrambled off his lap. "I—I can't. Sorry, I just..." What the hell was I doing? I couldn't even form a complete sentence. I was an excellent student. I'd been talking since I was two. I could figure out how to make my tongue form words. Right? "Where is my—" My voice trailed off as I looked around for my discarded dress.

There. I walked to the small pile of creamy material and lifted if from the floor. Holding it up, I shook out the non-existent wrinkles and realized I hadn't finished that sentence either.

Sex drunk? Orgasm overload? Did these Atlan guys

have some kind of magic pheromone in their skin that put their mates into a trance in which literally, the only thing they could think about was sex? And more sex. And skin and touching and big hands. Big fingers. Lips. Cocks. "Stop it!"

Kovo rose to his feet so quickly I barely registered the movement. He was at my side before I could blink.

Oh, shit. There would definitely be no outrunning this one. Ever. Probably not even in a car.

How did someone so big move so fast?

With a sigh, I placed one hand on his forearm and squeezed. "It's okay. I'm sorry. I was talking to myself. Everything is fine."

"No danger?"

"No? I was yelling at myself."

"No."

"I can't yell at myself?"

"No."

I looked up into his dark eyes and burst out laughing. He was dead serious. I was not allowed to yell at myself in his presence. "I'll try to remember that."

Still chuckling, I put the Atlan gown back on and felt a bit more like myself. Naked Adrian wanted one thing, and one thing only. More Kovo cock. Evil wench. Fully clothed Adrian would have to talk some sense into that bitch or we were not getting out of here, Kovo would be executed and I would never forgive myself. Or stop wanting him. Somehow, I knew no one else's touch would ever feel right after this. After *him.*

Hands on my hips, I paced. Turned.

Speaking of cocks.

"I can't think with your giant junk staring me in the face."

"Junk?"

God, he was adorable, in a big, beastly kind of way. I spotted his pants and walked to them. I picked them up and tossed them in his general direction. He plucked them out of the air without taking his gaze off me. Big, sexy and coordinated. If I could take him home, he would crush it in the neighborhood softball game. That would probably be cheating, but we tended to play with a loose interpretation of the rules anyway.

Squirrel.

Jeez. Focus here. And not on his hard cock. Or his muscles. Or what those thick lips felt like locked onto my—

You had that already. Down girl.

He watched me like I was a puzzle he had yet to solve. Good luck with that. I'd been working on it for years.

I moved in front of him and gently guided him back toward the bed. He allowed me to move him. Good thing, because if he didn't want to budge he was going *nowhere.*

"I think you're even taller than Max, and I didn't think that was possible."

"Who is Max?" His voice had an edge I chose to believe was protective and not jealousy.

"My stepdad. He's an Atlan, too. Can you sit down, please?"

He sat quietly and watched me with that stare I was beginning to like a bit too much.

"Can you please change back into Kovo? I really need to talk to him."

"No."

No? Was he serious? He had to go back to normal Kovo. Didn't he?

5

Adrian

"**K**ovo traitor. Lies."

Oh, shit. What? My mind was spinning with possibilities. Kovo lied? To whom? About what? Was that what the traitor comment was about? Because he'd lied? Would the beast admit if he knew Kovo had murdered someone? Did I want to ask him? Or should I wait and discover the details once I was out of here? There had to be an explanation for all of this.

I refused to believe my unlikely—virtually impossible —reaction to this beast was a mistake. Some kind of cosmic joke. I knew my own mind. I knew what I could and could not accept in a partner. Whatever twist of fate or improbable biology that was going on between us could not be a mistake. If he were evil I would know. I wasn't into psychic readings and Tarot cards and all that, but I did believe humans—and probably aliens—had a soul. Something bigger, and smarter, and much more aware than we were most of the time.

My soul would not be so cruel as to make me fall head-over-heels in love with a complete stranger, and then make him be what they said he was.

No. I could not accept that.

Whirling to face him, my words stuck in my throat at the sight of his hard cock leaning toward me, ready for round two. I hurried to him and grabbed the pants out of his hand. "Why didn't you put your pants back on? I can't think."

"Torn." He wrapped one hand around his cock, pumping his fist up and down to draw my attention to his —no. Not looking. *Not. Looking.*

Clothes. Torn. Right. He'd ripped them off his body right before he'd shoved that huge cock inside me and made me come over and over again.

With a nonchalance I was *far* from feeling, I arranged the pants over his hips and—other things—so that everything was appropriately hidden.

Except the bulge rising from the center of the small mound.

Hell. That was the best I could do. Now all I had to do was refrain from looking at his chest.

Screw that. Impossible.

I tracked down his shredded shirt, draped strips of it over his shoulders, gave up and yanked at the blanket on the bed. He lifted himself up enough for me to pull it out from under him. I wrapped it around his shoulders like a cape, covering as much of him as I could.

There. Much, much better. Maybe now I could think about something other than how much I wanted to take him for another ride. Maybe.

"Okay. Now will you please change back into your other self? Kovo?"

"No. Mine."

"What's yours?"

"Mate. You."

Oh, no. "Are you saying you are going to remain a beast forever and keep me for yourself?"

The heat in his eyes nearly made me swoon. That was *exactly* what this beast intended.

Was that even possible? Were there separate legal rights for a beast if his male counterpart committed a crime, but he did not? If the man—alien male—could be executed once the beast lost control, couldn't the beast be treated separately from the man in reverse? Especially if the beast had a mate?

I looked at the mating cuffs on my wrists. These meant something serious on Atlan. More than a wedding ring. More than anything humans could conceive of. This beast *couldn't* live without me now. I knew that much. His beast had bonded to me and only me. He was mine. He would do anything for me, to protect me, to keep me. Not just a promise made with words, but with thousands of years of evolution. With his body and mind and his soul.

His existence was tied to mine. If I died, he died. Where I went, he went. He would protect me. Love me. Kill for me.

In theory, romantic. Staring into the eyes of a beast you'd just met—and who you'd just had mind-blowing sex with? Totally different animal. Kitten to Bengal tiger level different.

Maybe I should have thought this through a bit longer before walking in here and getting naked.

I looked up at the clock, the ticking time bomb waiting to take my beast away from me. Thirty minutes, maybe less, and Stefani would be here.

I didn't have time to worry about every detail. He was mine now. That was something. Moreover, I wanted to keep him. Keep, keep him. Forever. Which made me just as wild and beastly as he.

A kitten didn't mate a tiger. If I wanted a beast, I would have to become one.

I was okay with that.

None of this made sense.

I was okay with that, too.

"Adrian." My name spoken in his deep voice made my nipples peak. God, I was easy.

"Beast."

"Come. Kiss." He held out one hand and beckoned me closer.

I took a step backward. Away from him. Drew breath to speak. His intoxicating smell made my knees week. Took two more steps. Decided to make it three, just to be safe. "I can't kiss you right now. My sister is going to be here any minute and we need a plan."

The beast chuckled. "My plan. Fuck. Scream. Come."

"You are a sweet talker, aren't you?"

"I feast. Sweet pussy."

Naughty. So tempting. Direct. My beast didn't mess around.

Said sweet pussy was wet as hell and in complete agreement with *his* plans. All of them.

I told her to shut the hell up, she wasn't in charge. She listened about as well as he did, adding a persistent throbbing to the wetness between my legs just to drive me to the edge.

Two against one wasn't even close to fair.

"I don't want them to kill you. Do you understand? I can help you."

"No help."

"What are you going to do? Break out of here? Go on the run like some kind of lunatic hiding in back alleys and trying to find some scumbag to smuggle you off the planet?" Every sci-fi movie I'd ever seen—which wasn't that many—was running through my mind. "No. I don't believe you did what they say you did. Why? I have no idea. I just know you didn't do it."

His response? Silence.

"Well? Did you do it? Did you murder someone and commit treason?" There. I could be direct, too. I had no idea what I would do if he said yes, he did all of it. He was a cold blooded killer and a traitor to his people, a cold-hearted bastard who deserved to die.

He didn't say anything, simply stared into my eyes with a blank look that gave nothing away. Nothing. Zilch. Nada.

"Damn it." I closed the distance between us and stood between his legs, our faces level with one another. "Tell me the truth. I'm your mate. Tell me. Did you do it?"

He blinked, slowly. "Kovo confessed."

My heart sank. "Kovo confessed? He admitted to all of it? Murder? Treason?"

"Yes."

"Didn't he know they would execute you?"

"Yes."

What was happening?

I leaned forward and rested my forehead against his, breathed him in. Something was wrong. This couldn't be right. Couldn't be happening. On the surface, every box was checked. The Atlans had a crime and a confession. "What about evidence? DNA? I don't know, footprints or pieces of clothes or hair? Surveillance videos? Do they actually have anything that proves you were there? Were you really there?"

"Yes."

Oh, god. "Why? Why did you do this?" If he truly were guilty, if he were a killer and a traitor, did I have the right to try to save him? To want him?

To love him? Did I love him? Already? Was that possible?

Was any of this possible? It felt like a lone rider on an out-of-control rollercoaster.

Nothing made sense. I'd been so sure I was right about him. So very sure.

And wrong.

Suddenly, I couldn't breathe. The room spun. I was hot, too hot. My skin tingled. My fingertips. The air was too hot. I was suffocating. My stomach heaved like I'd swallowed a large goldfish and it was trying to swim back up my throat.

No.

A large hand settled on my left cheek. A strong arm pulled my body against something warm and safe and comforting. Tears streamed from my eyes, slid down my cheeks, some making their way to my lips where I licked them away. Swallowed them down like bitter pills. Truth pills. I'd royally fucked this up. I couldn't even regret it. I'd been with him. I wore his cuffs. I felt like I belonged with him. He was mine. Even if it was only for a few hours, it was time I would never forget.

"I'm sorry. I'm so sorry. I shouldn't be in here." I whispered the confession against his lips right before I kissed him.

"No, you should not." A deep, angry voice startled me. My beast growled and rose to his full height, gently moving me behind him where I couldn't see a thing.

I didn't need to. I knew that voice. It was Maxus. Based on the sounds of pounding boots on hard floor, he wasn't alone.

"Adrian? You in there? Are you okay?" My mother's voice rang out like a bird's song in this strange and terrible place.

"I'm fine, mom." I called out from behind my mate's torso. I didn't want her to worry. "Don't hurt him. He didn't do anything wrong." I tried to step out from behind him, but my beast would not allow it. He growled a soft warning at me and used on arm to block my path.

"Stay. Protect."

"That's my mom. She would never hurt me. And Max is her mate, my father under Atlan law. I'm safe. It's you I'm worried about." I took another step.

"No."

"Kovo."

"No."

"Sorry, Beast, I have to—"

"No. Mine." He spoke to me but never took his eyes off our visitors. "Mate. Mine." He made the announcement and lifted both hands to show our visitors his mating cuffs.

No doubt, everyone could see them. And his chest. And everything else exposed when the haphazard coverings I'd made for him had fallen to the ground.

That gasp had to be from my sister. Maxus cursed. I heard shuffling and what sounded like weapons of some kind being checked. Turned on. Something. How many guards were out there now?

"Stef?" I called out.

"I'm sorry. I tried." She would have done her best to

hide, to buy me the time I needed. I knew that in my bones. I'd played my twin card, the once a year, not to be denied, favor of all favors to be used in the direst of emergencies.

For Stefani that had meant passing her university calculus class. Her last math class. Ever.

My request had been a lot bigger, sexier and more dangerous. But I hadn't cashed in a twin card in the last couple years. She owed me. Big time. But not anymore. Debt paid.

"Stef, how many are there?"

"Do not—" Maxus began.

"Eight."

Holy shit. Eight Atlan guards for one prisoner? For my beast? "Overkill, don't you think?"

"Let her go, Kovo." Maxus didn't raise his voice, which was a solid decision. Every muscle in Kovo's body was flowing, moving. Ready to spring.

"My mate. Mine."

"I am her father, Warlord Maxus. I served on Battleship Zakar for many years. I am a male of honor. I will protect your mate with my life. You have my word."

The beast did not move or speak as he considered Max's words. I placed my hands on the small of his back and stretched up on tip-toe to whisper to him. "It's okay. I promise. I should go with him. I will come back."

For about a minute I believed my mate would agree to let me go with my family. I meant what I said. I would be back. With a private investigator. A judge. A dozen lawyers. I couldn't just give up on him. I wouldn't.

"No. Stay with me. My mate. I protect."

I heard a deep sigh and knew, just knew, the sound came from Max. "I was afraid you were going to say that."

Kovo took a step forward, toward the front of the cell.

Max gave the command. "Do it."

The slight buzzing of the energy field went silent. Kovo roared. Whistling sounds pierced the air, followed by soft thunking noises.

Confused, I moved to my side to see eight huge Atlans shooting at my mate. Not bullets. Darts. They whistled through the air and sank into his flesh like toothpicks into a hot cake that was ready to come out of the oven.

Kovo managed another step. Two.

Three.

The guards backed up. Reloaded their weapons.

"Stop!" I yelled at them. Kovo had too many stuck in his body already.

"Indeed. That is enough." The strange voice drew my attention from my mate to another male who appeared out of nowhere to stand next to my sister. He was smaller than the Atlans, but not by much. His facial features were angular, the armor he wore easily recognized. He was Coalition Fleet. Military. And he wasn't Atlan, he was Prillon. I'd seen a few of them on Earth before mom and Max left the planet for good.

"Give him a minute. He will go down," the Prillon ordered.

Kovo growled, the sound the most menacing thing I'd ever heard. "Helion."

"Warlord."

"Kill you." Kovo snarled the threat seconds before he dropped, unconscious, to the floor.

The Prillon male raised a brow, no hint of amusement or enjoyment on his face as he looked at my fallen mate. "Not today, Warlord. Not today."

6

The Beast, Medical Treatment Cell

The Prillon warrior I'd served for years, the male who had forced me to make a terrible choice, sat next to the medical table I woke upon. Multiple heavy straps crisscrossed my torso, arms, and legs. I knew from prior experience that not even a Hive enhanced Atlan warlord could break them.

I knew because I'd watched this Prillon torture more than one for information.

Sometimes I'd helped, when the dirty work became too much for Kovo to stomach.

"Why here?" I asked.

Doctor Helion, Intelligence Core commander and overall pain in my ass blinked slowly as if confused by my questions. "What the fuck were *you* thinking, Kovo?"

"Not Kovo."

"A mate?"

Oh, yes. Adrian. I could still smell her on my skin. "Mine."

"Fucking idiot." Helion snapped to his feet like he'd been hit with a jolt of electrical current and began to pace next to my bed. "This changes nothing. Mate or no mate, you will be executed in a few hours."

"No."

"Yes."

"Mate. No fever."

"It's too late, Kovo. Too fucking late." The Prillon grabbed the chair he'd been sitting in and hurled it against the wall in a fit of rage. I had never seen him lose his temper. "Gods be damned, Kovo. You know what's at stake. Nothing can change. All you've done is ensure Adrian Davis will grieve when you die. That innocent young female will suffer when she should *never* have been involved." He walked to the chair where it lay on its side and kicked it. "Fuck. I have too many stains on my soul already."

"Mine." The fault was mine. I'd fought Kovo to be free. He knew the consequences of our actions, of our choice. He'd tried to deny me, the beast, the primal monster more instinct than male. "My choice."

"A reckless choice." Moving slowly, deliberately, he picked up the chair and brought it back to its original location near my head. He sat once more, outwardly cold as ice, and looked at me. "Beasts. You have no idea how many hours I have wasted trying to decide if you are all more trouble than you are worth."

"Battle." Nothing could stand before a fully armed group of raging beasts on a battlefield. At least nothing I'd ever seen.

"Yes. Which is why you are all treated like fucking kings, if you live long enough."

I turned my head and made a point of looking around. "Great castle."

"Indeed." He sighed, leaned back and crossed his arms over his chest. He wore black and gray battle armor typical of fighters in the Coalition Fleet. I wondered where he had come from in such a hurry that he had not changed into the standard doctor's uniform he often wore when in civilian areas.

I had always assumed he wore the green to camouflage the fact that he was every bit as much a killer as any beast. Wouldn't do to make people any more nervous than they already were when they had to deal with him.

"Kovo, this mission was simple. You volunteered."

"Not Kovo."

He narrowed his eyes and leaned forward to loom over me until our noses nearly touched. "Listen to me, beast. You are not separate. It's not in your nature. Kovo agreed to this. There is no going back. I came down here to make sure you understand what I am telling you. I am sorry you found your mate. I really am. But it changes nothing. You either break her heart or..." He leaned back again, sentence unfinished.

He didn't need to tell me what was going to happen. I knew.

I knew...and I regretted what I had done. Adrian was a worthy female. Beautiful. Soft. Perfect. She did not deserve the pain my death was going to cause her. I had lost control. Plain and simple. Now my mate would pay the price.

Fuck.

I closed my eyes and sank back inside Kovo. He fought his way to the surface, the change back to male at record speed. He was furious. In pain. Just like I was.

The only positive out of this entire situation was that we wouldn't have to suffer much longer.

***

Adrian, Warlord Max's Estate

The soft knock on the bedroom door had to be my mother. Stefani was already here, sitting on the oversized —Atlan sized—lounge that was puffy, soft, and large enough to hold four or five average humans.

"Come in." I stood before a large mirror. I didn't think it was an actual mirror, more like an advanced screen of some kind. It turned off when I wasn't looking, the floor to ceiling frame becoming a lovely piece of abstract art. I guess art was art, no matter what planet you were on.

"Girls, how are you?" Indeed, it was our mother. Alone. Which was rare these days. Guess that was to be expected when she was head-over-heels in love with Max. They were good together. Really, really good.

"This gown is amazing, Mom." Stefani waved her hand down over her torso to indicate the dark green gown she wore. This one was much fancier than the simple dresses we'd worn to the medical facility—make that prison—earlier. Same basic style, but these evening gowns had sparkling gold strands woven through the fabric in fascinating geometric designs. The patterns actually fooled the eye into thinking the lines were moving. It was totally amazing. I would have been excited about our attire—my gown was similar, but the base fabric was the color of yummy dark chocolate—except for the fact that I had on mating cuffs and no mate in sight.

Thank god the Atlans had updated their technology when it came to the cuffs. Apparently, the pain response programmed into the cuffs if a woman was separated from her beast was too strong for the human nervous system. So, they'd adapted the cuffs to make it possible to lessen the effect or turn it completely off.

I'd chosen '*off*' after the first zap had dropped me to my knees. My forearms still ached from the jolt I'd received when Max picked me up and carried me out of Kovo's cell like I was a misbehaving toddler.

I'd expected a lecture on the way home. I'd received worried looks from both Mom and Stefani, and stony silence from Max.

Of course, he was the Atlan. The big, famous warlord.

He was the one who was going to have to help me with this mess. Help me save Kovo.

Right? He *was* going to help me?

"Mom?"

"Yes?"

I turned away from the mirror, the dress and the fancy hairdo mom's attendant had insisted on unable to hold my interest. Stefani's hands were in her lap, locked together, her knuckles white. She looked gorgeous. Anxious. She didn't speak. Which was fine. This was my mess. My mate. My fight.

"How are we going to get Kovo out of there? They can't execute him now, right? He has me, a mate. He won't go crazy. They'll let him go? Do a retrial? Appeal? Something?"

Mom cleared her throat. That was never a good sign. "No. He is not there because he has mating fever. He is there because he committed murder."

"Who? Who did he kill? Because if it was some jerk, or drug lord, or criminal that deserved it, they should reconsider."

"You know that's not the way the law works, sis. At least not back home. Murder is murder." Stefani kept her voice low, almost a whisper.

I turned to my mother. "No one has told me anything. Not you. Not Max. Not any of the people who work in your house. Not that Doctor Helion creep. If Kovo's going to die, I have the right to know the details about what he supposedly did."

"Supposedly?" my sister asked.

I glared at Stefani. Sometimes it was uncanny, staring into a face exactly like my own. Sometimes, like now, I just wanted her to shut the hell up. "Yes. Innocent until proven guilty—"

"Which he has been." My mother took a seat next to Stefani as I walked back and forth, so agitated I felt like I had bugs crawling around between my skin and my dress.

"Guilty of what, Mom? They said he killed someone? Okay. That's what soldiers do. I just don't think he committed a cold blooded murder. That is a totally different crime. My gut is telling me something isn't right. Someone is lying. And even if Kovo did murder someone, I am one hundred percent sure they deserved it."

"That doesn't make sense, honey. There is no way you can know that."

I didn't dare look at my mom, didn't want to glare at her or give her the evil eye. She didn't deserve to feel the brunt of the rage I was feeling on Kovo's behalf. "Like there was no way I could have known he was my mate? That his beast would not only accept me, but want me so much he refused to transform back into his normal, Atlan self?"

"He did what?" My mom sounded shocked. "Is that why he was in his beast form when we all arrived?"

"Yes. The beast told me Kovo refused to claim me, even though he knew I was his."

"This doesn't make any sense." My mom, the queen of

this proverbial castle, stood and began to pace as well. Her gown was a shimmering wall of black that reflected rainbows of colors when she moved, like a dark opal. She was covered in expensive jewels and her mating cuffs had been upgraded as well. They were beautiful, obviously expensive, and one could easily argue they belonged on display like an ornate set of crown jewels.

I looked down at the plain, pewter looking cuffs on my own wrists and sighed. As a representation of the differences in our situations, nothing could have been more perfect.

Stefani shrugged. "Well, Mom, Max was so in love with you he hid the fact that he was an alien. He never let his beast meet you at all. You told me he was willing to live like that for the rest of his life, if it meant he could keep you."

"That was different."

"How?" I demanded. "How is that different, Mom? I have no idea how these guys go from man to beast and back again at will, but seems to me there is some kind of power struggle that goes on inside them. That's why they get locked up if their mating fever gets too bad. Their beast becomes more powerful, impossible to control."

"And turns into a raging killer." That was my sister. Pointing out the obvious. As usual.

"Not funny, Stef," I said.

"Doing my part for the stand-up comedy scene on Atlan."

"Well, don't quit your day job."

"Don't have one, so I'm good."

Usually charming but right now totally irritating. This was serious. "Just because Max figured out how to send money home and pay for school doesn't mean—"

"Enough." Damn that '*mom voice*'. Heard it since birth. My entire being reacted just like I had when I was three —straighten up and shut up. Vivian Davis had raised us alone in one of the worst neighborhoods in Miami. She didn't take bullshit from anyone. Especially not her daughters.

Tears threatened and I stopped walking, stopped moving. What the hell was I going to do? "I don't know what to do, Mom. I love him."

"You've known him for four hours." My sister raised her eyebrows. "The sex must have been amazing."

"Shut up, Stef."

"Girls," Mom said through clenched teeth. Unfortunately, my sister wasn't finished.

"Listen to reason, Adrian. How do you know he really cares about you at all? That you weren't just a sweet piece of ass offered to him at the last minute? Like his last meal?" She stood up to tilt her hip to one side so she could flop her arms around as she spoke. "Oh, sure. Uh, yeah, I'll have a filet mignon, rare, your most expensive wine, and, wait, one more thing. I'll take that nineteen-year-old hottie to sleep with, too."

"You're a bitch," I mumbled.

"I'm not. I'm your twin. No one else has your back like I do. And I don't like this situation. You played your twin card. Fine. I helped you get in there. Honestly, I figured he would either ignore you or tell you to get out."

"You didn't believe me when I said he was mine."

"Sorry. No. I didn't." At least Stefani seemed contrite about that. She lifted her shoulders in a slight shrug. "No one has ever heard of such a thing. It's weird. You acted like you were the beast, not him."

"I feel like one right now, let me tell you."

"If I'd known you would actually turn out to be his mate, I never would have helped you. Twin card or not."

"Why not?"

"Because he's locked up, waiting to die in the Atlan version of death row. You just told us you are in love with him. How could you be? I don't know, but whatever. It's worse for you if you *are* in love with him."

"How is that?" I asked.

"Because now, when they kill him, it's going to hurt you, too. Hot sex? Sure. He seemed like he was in control when you went in there. I never would have helped if I knew it was going to break your heart."

"They aren't going to kill him."

"Yes, honey, they are." Her mean mom voice was gone, replaced with soothing—I know it hurts but it will be better soon—tones. "His execution is to take place in less than an hour. Max received word a few minutes ago. That's why I came up here. I didn't want you to be alone when you heard."

"What?!"

"Calm down."

"I will not calm down!" I lifted the hem of the dress with which I'd planned to wow the biggest and most powerful politicians on Atlan and made haste toward the door. I had planned to spend the evening begging for Kovo's life. For help. For a stay of execution. New investigation. The list was long and nearly endless.

I had time for none of it if he was going to be dead in *an hour.*

"Adrian—" My mother followed behind me, Stefani behind her. We looked like sparkling ducklings all in a row.

I flung the door open and stormed past the two guards stationed outside. We were on Atlan, in Max's home, and he was *still* paranoid about our safety. For a moment I felt badly about the amount of worry I must have caused him when he found out I was in Kovo's cell. My remorse was quickly replaced with determination.

Damn it, Kovo was mine. My mate. Somehow, by some unexplainable miracle, I had known he was mine. That he wouldn't hurt me. That he needed me to save his life.

"Where is Max? Where is he? I need to talk to him right now. He has to help me. He has to." I would not cry. No. Would not. No panicking allowed either. None. I was the mate of an Atlan warlord. I had the mating cuffs to prove it. I wasn't a child. Not anymore.

My mother had to run to catch up, but she had always kept herself in shape so she could do her job back on Earth. Paramedics had to deal with car wrecks and unconscious bodies and all kinds of chaos. Mom could *run* if she needed to, and I wasn't all that fast.

She grabbed my elbow and pulled me to a stop. I swung around to face her.

"What? Where is he?"

"He's in his comm room."

"Comm room? Why? I thought he had that room built special so you could call us back on Earth."

"He did. And it cost a fortune."

Stefani finally caught up to us, not a hair out of place. No running for her. "Is he calling someone on Earth?"

"As a matter of fact, yes. He is."

"Why? Who is he calling?" I asked. My mate was in a running countdown toward death and Max decided to call another planet? And not just any planet, but Earth? What the heck were a bunch of humans going to do about an Atlan they knew nothing about?

"If you will follow me, ladies?" My mother walked as she talked, Stefani and I falling into step slightly behind her. "Doctor Helion is here."

"That asshole? What is he doing here?"

"Adrian, mind your tongue and your manners." Once a mother, always a mother. Well, at least our mother had her rules for operating in society. But this wasn't public, this was just us. I tried a different tactic.

"Kovo's beast threatened to kill him. I don't trust him."

"I understand. But Max does. And I trust Max."

Of course she did. She was his mate. And, to be fair,

Max was amazing. "That's not enough to make me like Helion."

Next to me, Stefani shivered. "He's ice cold. I'm telling you. Just standing next to him gave me the chills."

I huffed. "Talk about a killer."

"Ladies! Enough." Mom brought us to a stop in front of the closed door to Max's comm room. The door was thick. I couldn't hear a peep from anyone inside.

"Mom, just tell us what is going on." Stefani paused dramatically, eyebrows arched, and looked at me. "Twin, you keep quiet until she's done."

I rolled my eyes but said nothing. I was too anxious to argue. *Tick-tock. Tick-tock.* Every second we wasted in this house, Kovo was closer to gone forever.

Mom stepped in front of the control panel that would open the door and looked at us in turn. "Doctor Helion is here because he has a plan."

"What kind of plan?" I asked.

"Quiet, remember?" Stefani asked. I didn't even look at her, my full attention on my mother.

The door opened before I had an answer. Standing there was my stepfather, Max. Behind him, sitting at the comm station was the Prillon I'd met at the prison earlier. And on the large screen on the wall? A pretty woman I recognized very well.

"Warden Egara?" I swept past my mother and stepped around Max's oversized bulk, so accustomed to his size that I barely noticed. "What are you doing here?"

Well, not here-here, but she was *here*. Huge face, dark

brown hair, haunted gray eyes. She was young and beautiful but her eyes were old. Maybe she was one of those 'old souls' the psychics and Tarot card readers on Earth liked to talk about. Put on a hokey television show about paranormal phenomenon, and I was all in.

"Adrian. Stefani. I hear you have had an eventful visit."

Doctor Helion crossed his arms. "That, Warden, is quite the understatement. It's a fucking disaster." The Prillon studied me until I felt like an insect pinned to cardboard.

"Daughter." Max didn't raise his voice, but he definitely got my attention.

"I don't understand what is going on. We have to save Kovo. He doesn't have much time left." I was telling them something I hoped they already knew and agreed with.

Max held out his arm and my mother stepped in as close as she could get. They clicked, like two puzzle pieces designed to be together.

Like me and my beast.

"We are all here, Adrian, because Warlord Max has asked us to intervene." Warden Egara's familiar voice— I'd been at the Interstellar Brides processing center once a week to use their comm ever since our mom left the planet—seeped into my mind, slowly filling in the gaps until I could process what she was saying.

"He did?" I blinked, numb. Confusion warring with hope. I didn't want to be wrong, it would hurt too much.

"He did. And we have a plan."

Holy shit. Max? I hadn't even asked him to help me yet and he was already moving mountains for me.

Of course he was.

Tears burned on my lower eyelids but I ignored them to walk to my Atlan stepfather and give him a side hug. I could totally understand why my mother was so out of her head in love with him. "A plan for what?"

Doctor Helion scowled, his earlier neutral stare gone. "A plan to save your mate."

"What kind of plan?" I was glad Stefani asked because I couldn't seem to talk past the lump in my throat.

"An illegal one," said Warden Egara. For the first time I could remember, despite all the visits to the brides' processing center in Miami where she'd helped us talk to our mom, she laughed. "My favorite kind."

"I assume, Catherine, that after this we are even?" Doctor Helion stepped forward to stand directly in front of the screen.

Warden Egara's laughter faded as she looked directly at him and shook her head. "We will never be even."

After that curious statement, the screen went blank.

"Fuck." Doctor Helion turned to face my family and gave a slight bow to all of us. "I have people in place who will take care of this. Discreetly. Make sure you are prepared to receive the cargo when it is delivered."

"What cargo?" I asked.

"Kovo, honey," My mom whispered. "They are going to break him out of that place."

7

Kovo

     had ten minutes left. I had to figure out how to get out of these bindings, knock out the guards they would send to take me to the execution chamber, and fight my way out of here.

Just when I needed my beast to be a raging lunatic, he curled up in the corner of my mind and looked at me like I was the problem here.

You were the one who insisted on claiming her. He was not going to pretend this was my fault.

Mine.

We don't have a right to claim a mate.

Fuck Helion.

We made the choice.

You. Not me.

Would you rather we allow him to die?

The beast thought long and hard over this one, but I already knew what his answer would be. He claimed I had made this choice alone, but that was not the truth. We were one in mind and body. One being. One heart. We loved who we loved. We had made this sacrifice together.

We had fucked it up together, as well. Adrian. So small, fragile and feminine. So fearless. Standing there, facing us down with the courage of a warlord racing into battle. That alone had made my—our—cock hard before she'd dared take a step closer. That one step had sealed all our fates.

I should have fought you harder. Never touched her. I should have resisted. Been stronger. Fought the beast harder. When I'd needed to be stronger than I'd ever been before, I had failed. Failed myself, my commander, my beast and my mate.

Wanted her. The beast reminded.

We both did.

Mine.

"I know, beast. I know. Fuck." She was mine, too. The mating cuffs on my wrists sent shocks of sweet pain through every fiber of my being. That pain grounded me and my beast. We had a mate. The years we'd spent fighting and killing had built up a horrible rage. She was the balm. A new obsession. Our purpose. One we could not live without.

Not that we had much longer to live anyway.

I had no regrets in my life. None, except hurting her. Selfish bastard that I was, I couldn't even regret holding her. Fucking her sweet pussy. Tasting her wet heat. Kissing that soft mouth. The beast claimed her, but I had been there. Feeling everything. Taking everything in like the selfish male I'd turned out to be. Worse, I could not regret the experience. Hurting her? Yes. That was unforgivable.

But the beast was correct. We had both wanted her. I'd just needed to free my beast so he would follow instinct and claim her. Fuck her. Touch every soft, curved part of her. Taste her skin, her lips. Her pussy. Our mate's wet heat had set off an explosion of emotion neither of has had expected, nor been prepared to handle.

After that, we'd been truly lost to her. Anything she wanted, we would provide. Anything she needed. We would obsess over her happiness, her health, her smile. The beast lived to fight, but when the battle was done, when mating fever came for us, it was as if everything we'd ever done had to be atoned for, as if the only way to appease our gods was to serve our females. The flip of that switch, from predator to protector, happened in an instant. Pure instinct. Irreversible. Once we found our mate, there was no going back.

Not that any Atlan with a mate had ever *wanted* to return to his old ways. Fucking a beautiful, eager female was far superior to shredding Hive armies.

My cock grew hard as thoughts of her consumed me. I could still taste her. Smell her. Feel her smooth skin under my fingertips. Better to think about her in these last few minutes than about the fate that was coming for me.

Helion left earlier. I'd told him to apologize to Adrian for me, to beg for her forgiveness. I didn't deserve it, but I was going to stubbornly believe that with her soft heart, she would grant it regardless.

He had asked me the one question I could not lie about.

Was she truly mine? Did she calm the beast? Or had I claimed her in an attempt to escape execution?

As if I had no honor. I would never use a female in such a way.

I'd growled and the beast had surged back to the surface at his insult.

Fuck, yes. She was mine. How she found me in this place would always be a wonder to me, a mystery never to be solved. A fucking miracle. If a few hours of bliss was all I would ever have, then I would be grateful. Her mere existence brought me peace.

"Warlord Kovo." The door to the medical chamber slid open and four large guards walked inside. The two in front I recognized from their many visits checking on me, ensuring I was still alive so they could kill me at the proper time.The two behind I had never seen before. But then, I'd never been taken to the execution chamber, either. Had to be tough minded individuals to watch your Atlan brothers be put to death day after day.

"I am here. Where you left me."

The nearest guard, an honorable warlord named Lotte, and his counterpart, Trass, moved to stand beside me. They both looked down, inspecting the bindings.

Trass shook his head. "Dishonorable. You are not suffering from mating fever. You should be allowed to walk to your end with honor."

Lotte, a warlord who had served enough years in the Coalition Fleet I often wondered how long he would survive his own mating fever, grumbled agreement. "We have our orders."

"He is mated."

"The law is the law. He was convicted."

"Poor bastard. Killed his own brother."

"Quiet." Lotte glanced furtively over his shoulder as if he needed to ascertain the reactions of their two companions. "Half-brother."

"That warlord had no honor." Trass growled. "He did us all a favor."

Lotte's shoulders tensed, as if he were nervous. Were the two additional guards unfamiliar to Lotte and Trass as well?

"Shut the fuck up and get on with it." I didn't want to think about my brother, our fight, or the blood on my hands from countless enemies whose lives I'd taken in battle. I wanted to think about *her*. "I appreciate the sentiment my friends, but it's my duty to die today."

The true reason for my execution? No one but Helion, myself, and one other Atlan knew what really happened. No one else would ever know.

"Fucking stubborn bastard." Lotte slapped the center of his chest then closed his hand into a fist.

Trass did the same.

They both bowed their heads, honoring me in a way I had not expected.

"Thank you."

I closed my eyes and waited for them to take this bed —with me on it—to the execution chamber. There I would be sent into a calming sleep...and never wake up.

Whoosh.

Whoosh.

What the fuck?

I opened my eyes to see both Lotte and Trass glassy-eyed, darts sticking out from the sides of their necks.

Four more impacted their bodies somewhere I couldn't see. But I could hear them.

Thump, thump. Thump, thump.

The warlords crumpled at almost exactly the same time. The two strangers who had accompanied them caught them on their way down and quickly removed the darts, stuffing the evidence in their pockets.

"Who the fuck are you and what are you doing here?" I demanded.

The first walked around to the other side of my bed and started loosening the restraints. The second placed a hand on my shoulder and looked me in the eye. I knew that look. Deadly serious. No arguing. Resigned. Determined.

He was on a mission. Apparently, that mission was me

"Shut the fuck up and listen. Helion sent us. I'm Razz. This is Daan." The warlord jerked his head to the side to indicate his counterpart. "The vid feed to this room will come back up in approximately sixty seconds. We have a one-minute overlap programmed into the system that will turn off the security vids covering our exit route."

I stared at him, confused. What the fuck was Helion doing? My death was part of his plan. We'd spent weeks setting this entire mission up. He couldn't just fuck the whole thing up now.

The last restraint popped free and I sat up, swung my legs over the edge of the bed and then stepped onto the floor. My bare feet quickly found purchase.

Daan spoke for the first time. "You going to argue or get the fuck out of here and go to your mate?"

"They're going to have you on vid coming in here," I said.

"No they won't." Daan, who had been on the opposite side of the bed, headed for the door. He tapped the base of his throat and his image wavered like a mirage. "The vid will show two of each of them." He pointed to where Lotte and Trass lay unconscious on the floor. "Won't fool the eye, but will fool the vid monitors."

"Helion give you that?" I knew that fucker kept tech in reserve. This gadget would have come in handy on more than one of the special assignments Helion had delighted in giving to me.

"Let's go." Razz gave the order, not bothering to

respond to my question. Why bother? We all knew the answer.

Damn that fucking Prillon.

***

Adrian

If they were giving out awards for Hollywood level acting, I deserved one. So did Stef.

The reception going on inside Max's mansion was truly spectacular. Two days ago I would have been wandering with a joyful eye, in complete awe over the art and hanging lights. The glass? Maybe crystal? I wasn't sure, but the material was translucent and twisted into unique shapes that hung from the ridiculously high ceiling, each one of them longer than I was tall.

One side of the room was lined with buffet tables with every oddity imaginable. I'd tried a few Atlan classics. They weren't terrible, but I couldn't lie. I'd been really happy to come across the table that held Mom's selections. I'd never been happier to see chocolate chip cookies in my life.

There were other things, too. **Hors d'oeuvres** with cheese and meats. Stuffed mushrooms. Stuffed peppers. Jams, jellies, and baked goods to smear them on. There was even an ice sculpture—that didn't appear to be melting...at all—of a dancing fairy complete with pixie wings and adorable animals at her feet.

Not ice. No way.

And it sparkled. Stefani reached out to touch it as I watched.

"Looks like ice," she said.

"I think it's the same thing as the lights."

Stefani looked up, then back down. "Right. But I really wish Mom had chosen a bird or a waterfall or something. Do you know how many of these Atlans have asked me where the fairies live on Earth? And if they have mates?"

I chuckled because I'd been asked the same thing at least a dozen times. "I swear one of them looked like he was going to cry when I told him they didn't exist."

Stefani crossed her arms. "How do you know? Maybe they do. There are a lot of planets out there, right?"

"I can barely handle this one. If fairies are real, they're probably mean and like to eat small children." The half-eaten cookie had lost all appeal. I thought about hiding it on the table somewhere. Fortunately, one of the hired event staff appeared as if by magic and offered his tray as a final resting place for my unfortunate little friend. "Thanks."

Stefani watched the man—alien—walk away. He wasn't Atlan. None of the event staff were. They weren't human, either. I wondered where they were from. Another unknown planet?

Stefani interrupted my musing. "Eat small children? We're talking *Tinker Bell* here."

"Exactly. She turned out to be a jealous little bitch,

too."

"Jeez. Grumpy much?"

"I can't help it." I grabbed my second chocolate chip cookie and anxiously nibbled on the edge. If ever there was a day to '*eat my feelings*', today was that day. I felt like I was about to explode. Or sob. Throw myself down on the ground and have a massive screaming fit. I held all the emotions in. Barely. "Do you think they got him out?"

"Shhh." Stefani looked around. "You're lucky no one is close enough to hear you. Max told us, specifically told us not to say a single word about it. We are here so we can't be suspected. So is Max. And Mom. Even that scary Prillon doctor is over there chatting up some scarred-up Atlan who looks like's he's about a hundred years old."

"That's Warlord Zahn. He's the head of their war council." I looked at the older male, and the glittering mating cuffs on his wrists.

"How do you know that?"

I shrugged. "Couple days ago, I was excited about this party. I made an effort to memorize the guest list, like Mom wanted."

"Oh."

"Didn't even look at it, did you?"

"No." It was Stefani's turn to shrug. "I'm getting along just fine. No one expects me to know anything, so I just smile and pretend to be thrilled to meet everyone." She popped a pepperoni and cheese hors d'oeuvres in her mouth and grinned. "Nebe gonna tak tu thay pee-pu ebuh uh-gem."

I burst into a laughing fit, drawing the attention of several large males in the room. Shit.

I slapped my twin's ass behind us both, where no one would see. "Don't talk with your mouth full. God. You're a mutant."

She giggled. I scanned the crowd to find our mother watching us closely. She smiled and nodded, apparently pleased with our 'everything is perfect' performance.

Right. Perfect. Fine. Everything was fine. Everything had been lovely and wonderful for more than three hours now.

Except it wasn't. They'd forced me to remove my mating cuffs. Which made me sad, and angry, and finally resigned to letting go of my connection to Kovo for a few hours. A pair of mating cuffs on one of the human visitors under Max's protection would *not* be missed. Not only were we human, but we were his daughters. That would grant any mate of ours extra clout. Mating cuffs would invite our guests to ask questions. Lots and lots of questions that we would not be able to answer without ruining the entire plan to save my man.

We act normal or we ruin everything, according to Max. And Helion. And our mother. I sighed. "How much longer do we have to stay here?"

"Max said four hours."

"Shit." By my count it had been *maybe* three. And that was stretching it with wishful thinking and out-of-control optimism that I absolutely was not feeling.

Too many people. Too much talking. Too much noise

and light and people laughing while I was worrying myself to death on the inside. Had they reached the hospital prison in time? Had they saved Kovo or was he dead? If they got him out, had they been caught on the way here? Or was he somewhere in this mansion right now waiting for me? As I'd heard from my mother countless nights when we'd been late for curfew, '*You could have been dead in a ditch somewhere.*'

Like most self-absorbed teenagers, I'd believed her to be hysterical and over-reacting. I never took into account the fact that she put dead bodies in the back of her ambulance on a regular basis, some of them kids like us.

Guess the joke was on me. I got it now. I really did.

I owed my mother an apology.

"Is your inner introvert about to die in agony?" Stefani asked. "Mine rolled over and went belly up about half an hour ago."

"She is still upstairs hiding in the closet."

Stefani reached for my hand and entwined our fingers. I squeezed, thankful for the grounding and comfort she offered. We were twins. We knew more about each other than we ought to, that was for sure. Having someone who so completely understood me was amazing far more often that it was a pain. I loved my sister to death. I loved my family, my mom and my grandmother —when she'd been alive. I was learning to love Max.

And then there was Kovo, who was burning a hole in my heart with a blowtorch.

Did I love him the way I loved Stef or my mom? No.

This was totally different. This was obsession and lust. I seemed to be incapable of thinking about anything else ninety-nine percent of the time.

I would have entertained the idea that my single-mindedness might change in the future. Then I watched Mom with Max and knew I was kidding myself. This wasn't like falling in love with a human man, getting married, possibly divorced. This was forever. Until death. With an alien race so devoted to their mates, so dependent on their females to keep them sane, they wore mating cuffs that literally caused them physical pain anytime they were forced to be separated from one another.

And they *liked it.*

Was that love? My heart said yes. My head, however, thought my heart was a raging lunatic.

I sighed. "You should go dance, Stef. Maybe one of those hot warlords will catch your eye."

"No. No way. If I can't have Friday night hot wings at Richie's, I don't think I would survive." Richie's being her —well, *our*—favorite restaurant close to campus.

"Don't forget the ranch dressing."

"Blue cheese. What is wrong with you? You are a traitor to the true hot wing experience."

I smiled, but the attempt was weak and half-hearted. "Thanks."

"For what?"

"Trying to distract me." I scanned the crowd once more. There were fewer than a hundred people—Atlans

—here. We'd already met them all. Smiled. Made small talk for the required introductory period. Moved on. We were being watched, but we weren't being pursued. "Come on. Let's go to the kitchen and interrogate the event staff."

"What?"

"They're not Atlan. They're not from Earth. I want to know where they are from."

My sister sighed. "Can't you stop trying to solve puzzles for one night?"

"No." I was desperate for something, anything to distract me and Stefani knew it.

"Curiosity killed the cat."

"Idle minds are the devil's playground."

"That one is hands."

"Not for me. Not tonight." I begged her with my eyes to help me escape.

"Okay. But do *not* embarrass me. I do not need to see one of them naked."

"Can't let that one go, huh? I was eight."

"In the boys' locker room at the high school, demanding to see pubes."

"It's not like we had brothers. I needed to know." We didn't mention our biological father. Ever. He was kind of like that *Harry Potter* villain, *He-who-shall-not-be-named.* Our sperm donor had come from a rich family and demanded Mom get an abortion. She refused. He signed over rights to us and his family paid off my mom to ensure she never contacted him again. The only thing we'd inherited from him, or so we'd been told, was the oddly shaped birthmarks on our palms.

We *looked* like our mother. Thank god. I thought she was gorgeous.

Sperm donor's loss. Wherever he was, I was sure he was miserable. And alone.

We'd learned all the juicy details from our grandmother before she died. Mom was furious when she found out we knew. I was glad we'd been told the truth. Knowing my father was a complete ass was better than knowing nothing at all. At least I'd stopped wanting to meet him.

To this day I had never heard our mother speak his name.

Shifting our linked hands to linked elbows instead, I gently escorted Stefani in the direction I wanted her to go. I desperately needed a distraction so images of Kovo, writhing and suffering as they killed him, would stop racing around inside me like vultures waiting to feast on my dying heart.

So dramatic. So *emotional.* I might as well have thrown myself down on a stairway and gone for full drama like that Scarlett woman in the old movie grandmother had made us watch. More than once. Always causing trouble. Never thinking about consequences. Always emotional, stubborn, and playing the victim.

I had no idea why anyone liked that freaking movie. Seemed stupid to me. I'd never liked that woman. Only good part of that ancient movie was when Rhett had walked away and told her he didn't give a damn. *That* had been classic.

I stopped in my tracks. "Something is wrong with me." I was not a drama kind of girl. In fact, Stef was normally the one shouting and crying and having emotional meltdowns. Not me. Yet I'd been over-reacting to everything since we arrived on Atlan, like being here was changing my brain chemistry or something.

Vultures feasting on my dying heart? Really? Where the hell had that thought even come from? I was no freaking poet. I didn't think like that. I just didn't.

Stef came to a halt as well, since we were effectively tied together. "You're just figuring this out now?"

"Funny. I'm serious. I think I have an alien brain parasite or something. Or this NPU we got before we came here is doing weird things to my mind." NPU was short for Neural Processing Unit. It was the Coalition Fleet's version of a universal translator. It was small, but I could still feel the bump in the bone just behind my ear where they'd implanted it in my skull.

Stefani looked me over. Our gazes locked. "You're serious."

"I know."

"Shit." She took over, practically dragging me along. "Hurry up."

"Where are we going?"

"To find a doctor."

We made it halfway across the reception area, saying hello, nodding and smiling and avoiding being drawn into conversations about Atlan politics, the Hive war, and any number of other topics we knew absolutely nothing about.

We were brought up short by a wall of muscle. I looked up to discover Doctor Helion blocking our path. "Did I hear one of you say you need to find a doctor?" His gaze moved over us quickly, assessing. "What is wrong?"

"Nothing." Nothing I wanted him to know about.

"Something is wrong with Adrian."

Never had I wanted to punch my twin so badly.

"What is going on? Adrian, honey, are you not feeling well?"

Oh, shit. Was that my mom? I turned to find we'd drawn a smallish crowd. Even Max had abandoned the big war council guy to come toward me all big and huffy and worried.

"I'm fine. Just a bit of a headache." I was surprised to discover that was the truth. My head was pounding, literally *pounding*, like someone had set up a bass drum at the base of my skull and was playing a live concert with a heavy metal band.

"You're turning green," Stef informed me.

"Reflection off your dress." The room spun and I clung to Stef's arm so I wouldn't fall. Except something worse was about to happen. "I'm going to be sick."

By all that was freaking holy, I leaned over and vomited chocolate chip cookie sludge all over Doctor Helion's boots.

Kovo

The room they smuggled me into was nothing more than an I.C. bolt hole. Small bed, basic S-Gen machine, and a monitor I could use to see what was happening in the outside world.

They'd locked me into what amounted to little more than an oversized closet. Shoved me inside, told me to keep quiet, and locked me in. They called it a 'guest' room. I would never put a guest of mine in a room so small. I paced from one end to the other. Thirteen. Fourteen steps then turn. Back and forth.

Could I break down the meager door with one punch? Absolutely. Would I? That depended on how long they were going to leave me here.

Ten minutes ago, I was so thrilled to be alive and on

my way to Adrian that I vowed to wait in this tiny room as long as I must. Hours, if necessary.

Turns out, I was not as patient as I'd led myself to believe.

But then, the last few years, working with the I.C. and Helion, I'd become very skilled at lying. Even to myself.

Especially to myself.

Fuck.

The mating cuffs sent random jolts of pain up my arms, to my spine and down into my core. I needed them now like I needed air to breathe. I had a mate. She was real. She wanted me, too.

My beast's pacing inside my mind was far more violent than my outward appearance would indicate to others. If I was impatient, he was violently so. Demanding to know where Adrian was. Who she was with. If she was safe. Or crying.

Or naked.

My cock had been in a constant state of semi-arousal since she'd been forced to leave me. All I had to do was think of her and my entire being reacted. Beast. Man. Body. Soul.

If I still had a soul. Or a heart. I wasn't one to pray to the gods, as many in the Coalition did. Nor to the *All That Is*. The creator energy, the mother who had given rise to us all.

If praying would bring Adrian to me any faster, I'd be on my knees.

But it would not. I had to wait, as Helion instructed.

Wait for her to arrive. Hide until he could figure out a way to get us off this planet.

I turned on the monitor, eager for a distraction. All I saw were images of my face next to a warning to all citizens of Atlan. They had a raging, violent beast roaming the streets. The enforcement officer they interviewed instructed all citizens not to engage, but to call them.

I was to be killed on sight.

Fuck.

"Helion, where the fuck are you?"

As if summoned by will alone, a quiet knock sounded on the door. The space was so small a mere two steps brought me to the entrance. I activated the vid screen that would show me who was on the other side and saw her.

Adrian.

The beast surged forward.

Mine.

I told him to shut the fuck up, it was my turn and opened the door.

She stood small and alone in a stunning Atlan gown, rich brown laced with gold. She looked like a queen. My queen.

A flash of movement caught my eye, and I tore my attention from her long enough to see the same two males who had taken me out of the prison a few hours ago.

"You will be moved in approximately fourteen hours."

"Good." The sooner I got off this planet, the sooner I could start my life with my new mate.

"You got her?" Razz asked.

My beast wanted to answer them, so I let him.

"Mine."

The two Atlans chuckled and walked away. I was left staring down into the most amazing green and gold eyes I'd ever seen. She was even smaller than I remembered. Her dark red hair was styled as well, as if she'd been at a party.

"You are very beautiful."

Her cheeks turned a cute shade of pink as she looked at me. "Thanks."

I stepped back to allow her entrance into my kingdom, such as it was. She came inside without hesitation, which soothed a part of me I hadn't been aware was anxious.

The beast had fucked her. Claimed her. Spoken to her.

I had not. Would she accept me as readily? I did not want to say the wrong thing. Upset her. Frighten her. Make her angry. I had no idea what I *could* say. We were in a fucked up situation. I couldn't take her to dinner or to see my home planet. Atlan was a beautiful world, not unlike Earth.

"I'm sorry." The words came out of my mouth before I realized I was going to utter them.

She spun around, abandoning her intense inspection of the tiny space. "Why?"

"Why?" I closed the distance and reached for her, cradled her delicate face in my hands. I had to touch her,

I *needed* to touch her. "I am sorry I got you into this mess. I am sorry we were separated. I am sorry that the beast was so rough with you. I should have been the one to touch you first."

I kissed her then, gently, because I needed to taste her with my own lips, not *his*. "I should have been the one to fuck you." I kissed her cheek. She tilted her head to the side to give me better access and I took immediate advantage, running my lips down the curve of her jaw to nibble at her neck.

"Kovo. I was so scared when they took me away. I thought they were going to kill you."

They nearly did. A few more minutes and Helion's ReCon team would have been too late. That information was my burden to bear, not hers.

"I am here now. And I am never leaving you again."

She wrapped her hands around my wrists, not to push me away, as I first feared, but to lock me to her. My mating cuffs were on her wrists, the sight nearly driving me to pick her up, shove her against a wall, lift her skirt and fuck her mindless.

But that is what a beast would do. I was not a beast. Not today. Today I was a male who very much wanted to pleasure his mate. To savor her. Explore her body to the smallest detail. I wanted to claim every part of her with my hands. My lips.

My tongue. Gods, I couldn't wait to fuck her with my tongue, feast on her pussy, make her cry out over and over.

"Adrian." I held her head in place as I tasted. Plundered. Explored. Her small tongue met mine with a wildness I never dreamt possible.

"What?"

"I need to fuck you now."

She sighed with contentment, the sound so intimate and accepting it was as if she had been mine for years, not hours. The simple act stole my breath. "Don't you think we should talk first? The beast didn't have a lot to say except 'Mine'." She smiled against my lips. "He seems to have an unnatural fondness for that word."

It was my turn to smile. "Indeed. In that, he and I are one."

"Are you?" She tensed, her body changing from supple to rigid as she pulled away from me. "Are you sure about that? You didn't want me. You told me to get out of your cell." She wrapped her arms around her stomach and bent slightly at the waist. "Oh, god. I think I'm going to be sick again."

"Again?" What was wrong with her? Was she ill? Did she need a ReGen pod? Where was Helion when I really needed him. Fucking doctor. He was the only healer I'd ever known who had taken more lives than he'd saved.

"Just nerves. It's nothing."

"You were sick?"

"All over Helion's perfectly polished boots. Don't worry. I'm fine now. But his boots... I doubt they will ever be the same again."

Laughter burst out of my body like a cannon firing.

There was no holding it back. The very idea of the high and mighty, perfect killer having his boots covered in—well, I wasn't exactly sure what my mate had eaten—but whatever it was, I wish I'd been there to bear witness. "Mate, you please me."

"Because I puked all over Helion's boots? I couldn't help it. I was too nervous about what was happening to you. Wondering if they got you out in time, or if you were in that place dying alone because someone decided to do it early. Or what if they'd tried to execute you and they'd messed it up somehow? I saw this movie where the prison guard purposely didn't wet the sponge for this guy's head when they electrocuted him, and it was horrible. He just...burned or something. It was disgusting. And I kept thinking about you and—"

I pulled her to me and placed a finger over her lips. "I am very much alive, mate. No need to worry about me." I would make it a priority to discover what these *movies* were and their purpose. Were they educational material? Had she watched this during her schooling? More, I would chastise the idiot who had exposed an innocent female to such violence. "I can take care of myself. And I will take care of you."

She pressed her cheek to my chest, then lifted her chin, looking up into my eyes.

Gods, she was small. Fragile. I would need to be most diligent in protecting her. It would be my honor to do so, my reason for breathing.

"Are you sure? You told me to get out of your cell. You

refused to talk to me, let alone touch me. It was all the beast. Not you."

I lifted her, her bottom resting on my forearm, her arms wrapped around my neck. My beast, who had been fighting to come to the surface at her words, settled because we were holding her. "The beast and I are one."

"But—"

"No. No argument. We are one being. One heart. One mind."

"Then why would he touch me when you refused? I don't understand what is going on. He told me you tried to stop him."

I saw hurt in her eyes and I hated myself for putting it there. A true mate would never harm his female, physically or emotionally. I had failed her so much already. It was a wonder she was here.

"I was trying to protect you."

"Protect me? From what? From you?"

"No. I will never harm you. You are mine. I will protect you with my life and destroy your enemies. I will kill anyone who tries to harm you."

"That's a bit much, but I know. I've heard all this before."

"From whom? A beast has vowed to protect you? Are you his? His mate?" I would have to challenge this male. Rip him into small pieces. I would tear his head from his body and bathe in his blood. I would protect my mate. Mine.

MINE! The beast agreed. He was ready to go to battle. Now. Right fucking now.

"No. From Max. Warlord Maxus. He's my mom's mate. But now he says we are his daughters, so we are under his protection, too."

Daughters?

I had forgotten the other female, the one who looked like my mate but with brown hair instead of Adrian's red.

I preferred red.

I calmed as her words registered. The male in the corridor. The elder female who had called my mate 'baby girl'. Her mother. The pieces of what happened before my beast took over and fucked her—saturated our senses and our memory—slowly made their way back to me.

"If Maxus is your father, it was his duty to protect you."

"Was?"

"You are mine now."

Our faces directly opposite one another, my mate stared into my eyes. Searching for something. What did she need to find? Truth? Commitment? Obsession? Honor?

"I am yours, Adrian. Do you know what that means?"

"Yes. But you're mine, too. And...I have to tell you something. It's about how I found you. How I knew you were there. That you were mine. And it's what made me cover Helion's feet in chocolate chip cookies."

"You will tell me now."

"Don't get bossy. I already said I was going to tell you."

"Do not tell me that you will speak. Simply speak what I must know."

"Kovo, chill. It's not an emergency or anything."

"You do not understand me, mate. You are not my top priority, you are my *only* priority. Only you control the beast. He will no longer respond to me if you wish for something else. He is yours as well. I do not believe you understand the power you now wield. What you need, we will provide. What you fear, we will destroy. What pleases you, makes you come, makes you moan and sigh and beg..." I moved in close, my lips resting against hers, barely touching, teasing us both. "I live and breathe to make you come apart in my arms. I want your pussy tight as a fist around my cock. I need to fill you with my seed, taste you. You are mine and I will never get enough."

"God, you guys are intense. No wonder my mom—"

"Your mother? What about her? Does she require assistance?"

"What?" Adrian blinked slowly and pulled back just enough to focus on my face. "My mom? Oh, no. No, no, no. Never mind."

Her cheeks turned pink once more and I was coming to learn that happened when she was flustered on some way. "Very well. Tell me what I must know."

She looked around the room. "Don't you think this is weird? We're—well, you—are standing in the middle of a room just holding me in the air. It seems an odd place to have a conversation."

"Your slight weight is nothing. Do not fear you will fall. I can hold you this way for days, if you desire."

"Days?" She licked her lips and I wondered what she was thinking. "Really? Don't you need to sleep?"

"Of course. But if a mission is critical—as you are now of critical importance to me—I am capable of going several days without sleep."

She squirmed in my arms. The scent of sweet feminine arousal reached me. My beast breathed deep, taking in the familiar musk of our female.

Mate. Mine.

I know. Shut the fuck up. Our mate is trying to tell us something.

Want. Fuck.

If you ever *want to touch our female again, you will stop talking to me right fucking now.*

That must have worried him because he did not respond. But his driving, nearly out of control urge to lock his mouth over her pussy and taste her was driving me mad.

She cleared her throat. "Well, when I was feeling sick earlier, that creepy Prillon doctor—"

"Helion. Did he hurt you?" I would kill him. I would rip his arms from the sockets and watch him bleed out.

"No." She smacked my shoulder with a small slap of her hand that made my heart leap. She was not afraid of me. Not at all. Thank the gods.

"Then he may live."

She laughed out loud and I vowed to ensure she made that sound often.

"No, he didn't hurt me. Of course not. But he did put me in one of those coffin things, the ReGenerator or something?"

"ReGen pod. It will heal most injures, as long as one is not already dead."

"Ok. Whatever. He put me in one of those pods. I told him I was fine, but he insisted."

"Then he may live." Helion had cared for my female. He was a Prillon of honor. I owed him a debt.

Helion asshole. The beast chose the perfect moment to chime in.

Enough. She is speaking. And knock that off. My cock is throbbing and I can't think.

No think. Fuck mate.

Sometimes we have to talk to them first. Be quiet.

Fuck now. Talk later.

I chuckled at his proclamation. But what did I expect? They didn't call that side of us 'beast' without reason.

My beast grumbled, but the erotic images, the memories he was playing in our mind settled down to kissing her. Holding her small, naked body close, skin to skin.

Returning my attention to Adrian, I found her watching me silently, a grin on her face. "Is my beast giving you a hard time in there?"

My beast. He preened. I clenched my jaw. How the fuck was I jealous of...myself?

Still watching, Adrian laughed out loud. Again. She

lifted her hands to my cheeks and leaned forward, her small nose barely touching the tip of mine. "Are you in there, Cuddle monster? Is your Kovo being mean to you? Keeping you locked up and not letting you out to play?"

The beast purred. He fucking purred. I had never, *never*, heard that before. What the fuck was this female doing to us?

No, not us. Him. What had she done to him?

She stroked my cheeks for a bit and the beast felt as if he lay down inside my mind and stretched, loving every second of it.

"That's better, big baby. I'll deal with Kovo and I'll see you later."

Oh, fuck, did he like the sound of that. Images of thrusting into her while she had her back to the wall flooded my mind again. I nearly came in my pants. *Beast! Enough!*

He laughed. The beast fucking laughed.

As did my female.

"Why are you laughing?"

Her sparkling eyes focused on me. "Because you two are funny, arguing in there all the time."

I froze. "What? How do you know what my beast is doing?"

"Because I can kind of hear him. Not words, you know? Not like real telepathy, but I can feel his emotions enough to take a good guess. Right now, I'm guessing he is telling you to stop talking and get me naked."

"Yes." I wanted her so badly I didn't remember what

else we were discussing. All I could think about was my cock inside her, my mouth on her skin. Touching her everywhere. Making her cling to me in mindless abandon.

"And you are trying to be a gentleman."

Thank the gods, she understood. I answered through clenched teeth. I hung onto my control by a thread. "Yes."

"Don't."

"What?"

"I don't want a gentleman. I want you." She reached up and released the clasps that had been holding her gown in place. The dress fell off her shoulders, the clingy fabric stalling on the swell of her breasts. One tug, one move, and she would be bare.

The beast surged forward again, eager to take what she offered. I fought, hard.

No. This time, she's mine.

Mine!

Fuck. No wonder everyone believed Atlan beasts were savages. Absolute truth if they were all like mine. *She is yours. She is mine. She is our mate. We protect her together. We fuck her together. You already claimed her. The mating cuffs are on her wrists.*

The beast's smug satisfaction regarding that came through loud and clear. Luckily, it also appeased him and he backed off. I didn't want to focus on fighting him when I could be giving all of my attention to our mate.

I shook my head to clear him from my mind and

found our mate watching me once again, a knowing grin on her face. "Did you two get it all figured out?"

"Yes."

The moment the word left my mouth, my lips were on hers. I was not a beast, not an animal. I wanted our mate soft and open beneath me. I wanted to take my time, taste all of her.

I carried her to the small bed and laid her down on her back. The soft slippers the females wore were the first things to go. I kissed her bare ankles, the heat of her core calling to me.

Pussy. Hot. Wet.

Mine.

The primitive desire to conquer her was not coming from my beast this time. The need to possess her, fuck her, sink into her body, was all me. I was nearly as animalistic as he.

I kissed a trail from inner ankle to knee. Thigh. Her scent tempted me to hurry. I would not. I took my time, kissing and tasting her. Moving my hands up her outer thighs, I slid the gown up and out of my way until the fabric covered her hips. The sight of her core peeking out from under the glittering fabric made me shudder. That was mine.

When I could not wait another moment, I lifted her ass in my hands and lowered my lips to her clit. One gentle kiss made her whimper. The beast stirred, eager for me to get on with it. I sucked on her sensitive nub until her hands were fists in my hair and her back arched up off the bed. She was close.

I smiled. *Not yet, mate. Not yet.*

Leaning back on my knees next to the bed, I pulled the gown off her body and quickly stripped off my own clothing. Skin to skin. That is what my beast wanted. That was what I needed. Her scent on my skin, part of me. Her declaration that I was hers. A male who smelled of his mate was accepted. Claimed. Loved.

Worthy.

I had given up hope, agreed to Helion's insane plan. All because I'd resigned myself to never finding or claiming a mate. Never finding *her*.

She reached for me. "Hurry up. How many clothes are you wearing?"

I lifted her off the bed, repositioning her so I could cover her with my body. Shield her. Protect her. Feel, for the first time, that she was safe.

She opened her legs wide and wrapped them around me the best she could as I kissed my way up her belly to her breasts. I stopped there for several minutes, unable to decide which one was more delicious.

"Kovo." She whispered my name. Hands buried in my hair once more, she pulled me up, lifted her head off the bed to capture my lips with hers.

She kissed me. I had never been kissed before. Not like this.

She held nothing back, wrapping her arms around

my neck and plunging her tongue deep in challenge. My mate let me know exactly what she wanted.

My last coherent thought as I plunged my cock deep was that I was lost. Gone.

Hers.

Deep within, the beast laughed at how easily she had conquered me.

9

Adrian

weet mother of God. The beast had been wild.
Rough. Raw lust personified.

This?

Kovo shifted his hips again and I moaned. So close. I
was so freaking close. I held my orgasm back, allowed it
to build, as I suspected he was doing.

The moment stretched like a shift in time and space.
Nothing else existed. Just us. Here. Now. I was having sex
with my mate for the first time. This was *different.*

This was emotions and commitment. We weren't in a
prison any longer. He wasn't about to die. He was going to
live a full life. Helion was going to get us off the planet
somehow. I was going to be able to keep him.

He wasn't going anywhere. He was mine. My mate.

I was married now. More than married. I had a *mate.* Forever.

A wall of chaotic emotions welled up from the base of my ribcage, moved up through my chest to my throat, to my eyes. Tears leaked silently from the corners, slid to my temples, and disappeared in my hair. I didn't know why I was crying. I just knew as his body moved over me, that loving like this *hurt.*

Agony had never been so wonderful.

Kovo moved faster. I tilted my hips so he would hit just the right...spot.

His chest was gorgeous. Muscled. I lifted my hands to lay them flat on his skin and moved them up and down over his bulging shoulders. He held his body a fraction above me with heavily muscled arms, the cut lines of his strong body drawing my eye like magnets.

I couldn't get enough. I wanted to hug him, bite him, squeeze him, moan, scream. Everything combined inside me until I exploded.

He fucked me through the orgasm, the slide of his huge cock stretching me open, filling me to the brink, hitting the nerves again and again until I thought I might die from orgasm overdose. I didn't know how much violent pounding my heart could take.

A few more thrusts, slower, deliberate, and Kovo joined me. His hands clenched into fists and pulled up the blanket next to my head.

I stroked his chest until it was over and he could focus again. Our gazes locked. I licked my lips.

His cock twitched inside me. "Careful, mate."

"Or what? You'll make me have another orgasm?" I couldn't seem to stop petting him. Didn't want to. "Perhaps I should warn you now. That is not a very effective threat."

He stared at me for a few seconds then burst into laughter. He rolled to his side, pulling me with him so that we were both on our sides, facing one another.

We remained silent for long minutes, coming down from the edge. His huge hand moved at a soothing speed from upper thigh, over my hip to just beneath my breast. Over and over until I was touch drunk.

"What were you going to tell me?"

"Hmm?" Words? He wanted me to use words? Now?

He stopped petting me and I opened my eyes in instant protest. "Don't stop."

"You seem unable to talk when I touch you."

"I can talk."

He ignored me as if I hadn't spoken. "An interesting and powerful fact to remember for later."

I scoffed. "You cannot just pet me to get me to—"

He cupped my breast. I sank into the contact, melted into a proverbial puddle.

Fuck words. Who needed 'em?

He chuckled and removed his hand, leaving me feeling chilled. Which, of course, made my nipples get hard as little diamonds. Traitors. "Now I'm cold."

His response was to pull me closer, lift the blanket

behind me and wrap it around me until I was like a little burrito lying next to him. "Better?"

"Not as good as you petting me." No sense lying. Not when I wanted his hands on me as often as possible.

God, this mating thing was intense. I never would have understood it, not really, if...

"What is it? You must tell me." Kovo's deep rumble turned serious. "I cannot protect you if I do not know what you must face."

I sighed. "It's nothing like that. It's just, it's kind of a shock. Stefani is more freaked than I am. But, I have you now, so..." My voice trailed off. It wasn't that big of a deal. Right? He wouldn't care. He totally wouldn't care.

I cared. I had always hated the part of me that had come from my father. Never understood why he'd acted the way he did with mom. Never even asked to see us. And now, thanks to *him*, I had Kovo?

I had to be grateful to my deadbeat, absent, never bothered to meet us, father? That just would *not* compute.

Kovo waited. He reached up with one hand and slowly traced my cheekbones with one fingertip. "You are very beautiful, mate."

"Thanks." Mom had always taught me to simply say thanks when given a compliment, even if you didn't believe it was true. Not that I was ugly. I was okay. Kind of average. I had the red hair, which was actually nice. It was more auburn and less carrot-top. But with it came the skin so pale it showed every scratch and bump and pimple I'd ever had. I was getting freckles on my arms and back from the days I'd spent on Florida's beaches. I was no runway model. Not skinny enough for that. Not tall enough either. I was a whole lot of average.

Judging by the total devotion in Kovo's eyes, he meant every word. He thought I was beautiful. That was good enough for me.

"Are you ready to tell me what troubles you?"

"It's not trouble. It's just unexpected. That's all. But it does explain how I found you and knew you were mine."

He stilled, his attention instant and intense. "How did this miracle occur? The beast always finds his mate first."

I had to wiggle my arm free from the burrito blanket. Arm free, I tucked the top of the blanket back around me and held up my hand, palm out, for Kovo's inspection. "Look at my palm. See anything?"

"Your hand is very small."

"What else?"

"The fingers could be broken with very little force. The nails are not long enough to cause more than surface damage, although your fingers are long enough to go through an opponent's eye and reach the brain as long as your opponent is not in beast mode. In that case, I believe your finger would blind him but fail to reach the brain."

Had this Atlan spent his entire life assessing enemies and killing things or what? Jeez. How sad. That life was over. No more.

"I'm talking about the little mark in the middle of my palm. Have you ever seen anything like it before?"

He glared at my hand as if it were a total puzzle. "It resembles the Everian mark, but is not as large, nor complete."

"That's because my dad wasn't a full-blooded Everian. He was only half."

"Your father was an Elite Hunter?"

"No. Apparently, my grandfather was. He did a mission on Earth about fifty years ago."

Kovo bristled. "He abandoned his mate and child?"

I sighed. That was the first thing Doctor Helion had said when he saw my DNA results on the medical scanners. "No. That creepy Prillon doctor, Helion? The one you threatened to kill?"

He chuckled. I failed to see what was funny.

"He must have a lot of super top secret clearance or he's a really good hacker."

"What is a hacker?"

"Someone that can break into computer programs that they aren't supposed to be able to get into."

When Kovo nodded but didn't say anything, I continued with the relevant part of my story. "I'm part Everian. They have this weird psychic connection with their mate when they are close enough. Helion said it's usually only between Marked Mates, where they are both Everian and their birthmarks have some kind of funky connection. But, for some reason, that part of my brain— the *alien* part—decided you were mine. So now, I can sense some of your emotions. Especially when you are in your beast mode. Probably because he's not as—"

"Good in bed. Capable of feasting on your pussy to make you scream?"

A stirring in the back of my mind that I now recognized as my newly discovered Everian psychic abilities, alerted me to the beast's irritation with Kovo's claim. I smiled. "He thinks he can do better."

"I know."

I wasn't quite ready for another wild ride so I snuggled deeper into my burrito blanket and pressed my body as close to Kovo as I could get. Laying here with him felt safe and warm and cozy. Perfect. He felt perfect.

I tried to focus on my contented feeling and hoped whatever the odd connection I had with my beast might be, he would feel my languid state and calm down.

"You did hear that part, right? About me being an alien?"

Kovo looked at me, confused. "You are no more alien than you were before."

"Yes, I am. I was human and now I'm one quarter from another planet."

"You are not Atlan. You are one hundred percent alien to me. It matters not what planet, or planets, you come from."

I *was* the alien here. Holy shit. That was freaking weird. Of course I was the alien. Why hadn't I thought of that before?

Cool. I was an alien. "If I'm an alien now, can I have one of those cool blaster guns I've seen? I think they would be really fun to shoot."

"No."

"Do you have anything like the light sabers in *Star Wars*? I've wanted one of those since I saw the new movies. It's a sword made out of light that will cut through anything."

"Absolutely not."

"Do you have a spaceship? Can you take me flying?"

"I do not own my own ship. Perhaps I can arrange a trip for us. Once we are free."

I'd completely forgotten that he was a wanted murderer who broke out of prison and had the entire planet hunting for him. I contemplated our not-so-guaranteed future in silence, comforted by Kovo's renewed stroking of my back, his steady breathing and his heat. No teddy bear had ever been this good.

"What are these movies? You repeatedly mention them."

"You don't have movies? They are stories on video. Real people, well it can be cartoon characters, too. They act out a story and people watch it."

He said nothing for a few minutes. "I would like to see this thing. Movies."

"I'll take you sometime. We'll get a large popcorn, load it up with butter, and toss in some candy."

He looked down at me, our gazes locked, happiness in his eyes that I was very sure was also reflected in mine. "I understand half of what you say, but I will trust you, mate, not to poison me or lead me astray."

"Deal." I chewed my bottom lip and tried to decide if I

was ready to know the answer, or if I should keep my mouth shut.

Damn it. I had to know.

"Kovo, why were you in that prison cell? And don't tell me it's because you killed someone you weren't supposed to. I do not believe that. I am calling bullshit. So tell me the truth."

My emotions flashed with dread, made my head and heart heavy. Not me, the beast.

"And why is your beast so upset about it?"

Kovo sighed. "You are my mate."

"Yes. I am. I'm not giving you up. My Everian brain decided you were mine, so I'm keeping you."

"As my beast has claimed you."

"Sounds like a plan. But I need to know what is going on with you. I don't believe what they said about you. It's impossible."

"I have killed many times. Why is this so difficult for you to believe?"

I wanted to slap him. He was evading. "Enemies don't count. Bad guys don't count. War doesn't count. Soldiers follow orders. I understand that. But when I had to leave you, they showed me your records. It says you killed your own brother."

"I do not wish to speak of it."

"Tough. I want to know. I need to know."

Kovo rolled off the bed and reached for his pants.

"Where are you going?" I asked.

"I cannot hold you and speak of such things."

"Okay." I watched him pull his pants up over his hips. His legs disappeared. His cock disappeared. Damn. But I could still see those ripped abs and massive chest. Plus, he was barefoot, which somehow made him adorable. Not that I would ever use that word out loud. It would be like telling a crocodile it was cute while it was trying to pull you down to the water, roll you under and feast on you later. Not the best plan.

He paced. I admired. I could do this for hours, content to watch and wait.

"I joined the Coalition Fleet young. I fought on the front lines for several years. Killed many enemies. I was always one of the first to change back to my normal form after a battle."

"You mean you'd fight as the beast and then change back into your normal size?"

"Yes. It is difficult when you have been killing, when the stench of blood and death surrounds you."

He ran a hand through his hair, a nervous gesture I had never seen before. I catalogued it for later. I had a lot to learn.

"For some unknown reason, I have always been able to control my beast far better than most."

"Stubborn," I muttered.

"What did you say?"

"Nothing. Keep going."

He glanced my way twice more before continuing with his tale and his pacing around the small room. "After a few years, a senior warlord approached me. I cannot tell you his name. He told me they wanted me to join the Intelligence Core. The I.C., as we call it, handles difficult missions, rescues, assassinations. We are spies and hunters. Mostly, we hunt. And we kill."

"Okay. So you were really good and they wanted you to join their Spec Ops."

"Spec Ops?"

"Special Operations. It's what Earth military call their best soldiers. They do all that stuff you just said."

"Very well. Special operations for the Coalition Fleet. I was honored."

"You said yes on the spot."

"Of course." He stopped looking at me and I braced myself for the difficult part of his story. "My brother, Reji, is three years younger than I. He joined the Fleet as soon as he was able. He was an excellent soldier and gained Helion's attention quickly. As soon as Reji had the required service time, Helion recruited him into the I.C. He was proud to follow in my footsteps."

"You were a good big brother."

"No. I was not." He placed his hands on his hips and scowled at the floor as he walked back and forth, back and forth. "I should have forbidden it. I knew what he was going to be involved in. I knew the danger he would be in. I made a weak attempt to talk him out of it, but he laughed, told me not to worry, and joined Helion the next day."

I had no idea where this story was going. "You love your brother."

"Yes."

"So what happened?"

"Helion. That's what happened. Fucking bastard. I should have killed him, but he had no choice. None of us could come up with a better solution. His idea was the only one that would save my brother's life."

"But, they said you killed him."

"I know. Helion needed him to be dead, so we faked his death. It had to be real. Undeniable. No one could suspect."

"What? Why?"

He ignored the question. Kept talking. "I had been tested for a bride more than three years ago. I had no match. No hope. Mating fever grew stronger every day and I knew I was close to losing control of my beast. Once that happens..."

"You're executed."

"Yes."

"So you let them believe you killed your own brother because you were going to die soon, anyway?"

"Yes. His mission is of vital importance. I was dead already, barely hanging on. One way or another, it was going to be over soon."

"Let me get this straight, Helion convinced you to pretend to kill your brother for some secret mission, make yourself a pariah to your entire planet, where everyone now hates you and thinks you are a horrible person, all because you had mating fever and gave up on finding a mate?"

"Yes."

"So, take it back. Tell the truth."

He laughed, but there was no humor in the sound. "The evidence was carefully planted. I confessed to the crime. Everything they discovered confirmed my version of events."

"Except the dead body. Where was that? If he's not dead, where did they get a dead body?" No body, no crime, right? I watched crime shows so much I firmly believed I could be a homicide detective. Which I believed I would enjoy until I did a ride-along and saw a corpse in person. The smell. The way the body looked?

No. I couldn't do it. No way.

"Reji was a member of the I.C.. Helion himself led the investigate."

"And planted all the evidence. Made sure everything pointed directly to you."

"We took blood from Reji minutes before we put the plan into action. Positioned a spray so that it would appear that I had attacked him from behind, knocked him to the ground and then killed while kneeling over his body."

"You guys faked blood splatter patterns? With real blood?"

"Yes."

"That insane. You know that, right? What was so freaking important that you did all of this?"

"I cannot tell you details, mate. It is bad enough that

you know Reji is alive. If that information became available, his life would be in danger."

"So, he has to officially stay dead because now he's on some super-secret mission and no one will suspect who he really is."

"Yes."

"And you were supposed to be executed. Case closed. No one would ever suspect a thing."

"Yes."

I sighed. Holy. Shit. "Then I showed up and ruined your plan."

"Yes. Helion was not pleased."

Bastard. I bet he wasn't. "Couldn't he find some other way to fake Reji's death? Shoot his body into space or something? Say he was killed in battle?"

"No one could question his death. He could not simply vanish. We needed evidence. Blood. A raging beast lost to the scourge of mating fever. A thorough investigation that Doctor Helion led himself. A public display. We could not risk anyone hiring Elite Hunters to track him. They are...very good at what they do."

"Everian Hunters?"

"Yes. They have a sense even they do not understand. If they are on a hunt, they can sense the direction their prey traveled. Sense their presence. I do not not how their gifts work, but I have been with an Elite Hunter while he was tracking an enemy. The experience was enlightening."

"But the I.C. planned the fake murder in the first place."

"One of Helion's top officers was murdered by his own brother, a raging beast. The story traveled to every trading station, every planet in the Coalition."

"You weren't out of control."

"If you watch the arrest vids, you will see a very different beast from the one you know." He looked at me, finally, and I could not bear the pain I saw in his eyes.

I could imagine the act Kovo had put on for the world —more like the universe. And no, I did not want to witness any such thing. "Someone really horrible must be hunting your brother."

"Not anymore." Kovo walked to the edge of the bed and sat down, his hip next to mine. "No one hunts for a warlord who is already dead."

"And you thought you were going to die anyway, so why not use your death to save him."

"Now you understand. I cannot tell the truth. I must never reveal that Reji is alive, or he will be hunted."

"Where is he now?"

Kovo shook his head slowly. "I do not know. Helion told me Reji is on a mission. I did not ask for details. Helion would not give them to me, and I do not want to know."

"You would worry about him."

"He is my brother."

"I'm sorry."

"If I had known about you, mate, I would not have agreed to Helion's plan."

I took his hand, pulled it to my lips and kissed him. "What would you have done? You had to save your brother."

He shrugged, his gaze locked on the place my lips rested against his skin. "A mate is everything. I would have found another way."

I believed him. "So, if our mating is going to totally mess up Helion's plan, why is he helping you? Why help you escape?"

"I do not know. He was enraged when he found out about you."

My turn to shrug. "Well, you're mine now and I'm not giving you back."

My words pleased him. He bent over to kiss me. I met him halfway, the blanket falling away to reveal my bare breasts.

It was a long time before I had room in my mind for anyone but him.

10

Kovo, Two Days Later

I woke with my mate curled against me in a comfortable bed. I treasured the last two days spent alone with Adrian. As much as we wanted to pretend the outside world did not exist, we both knew this interlude would not last.

She worried. As did I. I knew the way Helion worked. I'd been following his orders for years. It was not typical of him to delay an extraction. And this location?

Quiet.

Too quiet. Especially this morning. Something felt...wrong.

The moment the thought entered my mind my beast fought to break free.

Danger.

His terse tone left no doubt he sensed something I did not. *I've got this. Tell me what you know.*

Quietly, I slipped into my gear. I was prepared. I had used the S-Gen machine to create the armor and weapons I normally used. The S-Gen machines were typically locked, unable to produce such items. I, however, was I.C. and knew more codes to bypass these kinds of locks than any criminal. If I'd wanted to walk away from the I.C. and start a criminal gang, I could have done so at any time.

As gently as possible I touched my mate on the shoulder and woke her up.

The moment she saw me, she gave me her sleepy smile and reached for me. "Hi."

"Hi." I had grown accustomed to her human greeting. Found it suited me.

She blinked a few times, looked at my gear and sat up. "What's going on?"

I placed a finger over her lips so she would know to speak quietly and leaned in close to her ear. "The beast senses danger. I do not know yet what I will be dealing with."

"You mean we. What we'll be dealing with."

We'd had this argument multiple times during our brief stay. "No. I do not. It is my honor to protect you."

"I'm your mate. I get to protect you, too."

"My love, it is not necessary. I will not allow you to be hurt. It is too dangerous." I rose to fetch the clothing I'd made for her. It wasn't a flowing Atlan gown, as we would likely be traveling. Instead, it was a lighter version of my armor. Rather than black and gray, the material was green and gold, like her eyes. I helped her dress and brought her boots. She put those on while I dug through the pile of mistakes—this space did not have a working recycling unit—and pulled free the shoulder wrap I had created. The fabric was long enough to tie into a loop over her shoulder when she did not need the warmth and pull free to wrap her upper torso when she was cold.

I had been awake for hours contemplating the responsibilities I now had and how best to take care of her. My beast gave me several ideas as well, although they all were related to pleasuring her. Part of me truly was an animal.

Not that she would mind. I had a feeling she would love every idea just as much as I did. The beast seemed to cross his arms with a very arrogant satisfaction. He knew her as well as I. Perhaps on a more basic level.

"What's so funny? Beast is very pleased with himself. Worried. Pleased. Worried. What is it? Do I look weird in these clothes? What did you make for me anyway? I look like a *Star Wars* character. All I need is that ray gun."

She stood before me looking...beautiful. Stunning. Mine.

"Hint, hint, Kovo."

"No weapons."

"You're a weapon. Does that mean I can't have you?"

"I am the ultimate weapon, female. You need no other."

That made her laugh.

"You are so beautiful. I want to strip that armor from your body and fuck you again."

She grinned, shook her head, and blushed—a term she had taught me to explain the pink tinge that colored her cheeks when she was embarrassed. "We barely got out of the shower a few hours ago."

"I know."

"We've had sex at least a dozen times."

"Not enough." I stepped forward to gently lift her face to mine with a finger beneath her chin. "I will never get enough."

Loud pounding sounded on the door. Adrian gasped and swirled to face the entrance. Quickly, I positioned myself between my mate and whatever was on the other side of the door.

Whoever it was pounded again. "Warlord Kovo, we know you are in there. Surrender, sir, or we will have to take you by force."

My beast growled at that, more than ready to kill anyone who came through that door to threaten my mate.

Moving quickly, Adrian stepped up to my side. "I'm going to answer that and tell them to go away."

"No. They will not believe you. One of them would put his hands on you and I would not be able to control what happened next."

"Oh." She glanced up at me and placed her hand on my arm. "That bad? Really?"

Contemplating how to explain the ferocity of my instinct to protect her without frightening her, my beast surged to the surface. Impatient fucker.

"MINE."

Adrian's eyebrows shot up. "Okay then. That bad."

The beast receded, satisfied that she had received the message. However, he did not go dormant. He waited. We both knew what was on the other side of that door for me.

Death.

"Kovo."

"Yes, my love?"

She blushed again at my words. I found every opportunity to put that shade of pink on her cheeks. "You know who got you out of there once. Couldn't he do it again?"

"Perhaps." The vid reports I'd been monitoring while Adrian slept had repeated over and over the news of my escape. There had been no mention of the two who had come for me. As far as the public was concerned, they still had no idea who had helped me escape, nor why.

I picked up the helmet I'd set aside and activated the neural link. The familiar scan and sensor data streamed into my mind, the display in one eye showing me real time information.

"Fuck."

The entire building was surrounded, at least twenty warlords waiting for orders. There were two beasts at the door with six more down the hall, waiting to rush me when the door opened. Twenty-six trained warlords. All for me?

My beast snorted as if to say, '*Damn right. Should have brought more.*'

Only that animal could make me grin at a time like this.

Adrian walked into my arms, pressed her body to mine and wrapped her arms around me. Just for a moment. "What are we going to do?"

"There are almost thirty warlords here to take me in."

"That's crazy. Why do they need so many for one person?"

"MINE." The beast's voice spilled from my throat.

"Oh."

I leaned down and pressed a kiss to her lips. Perhaps my last one.

The thought made me linger as she melted against me.

"Warlord Kovo! You have a count of ten to open this door. Ten. Nine—"

I set Adrian away from me, pointed to an out of the way corner where she would be safe, and transformed.

The door burst inward, no doubt the result of a beast's fist ramming through. I waited as the door skidded across the floor, the top edge sliding to a stop at my feet.

"Kovo, we are coming in. We have orders to kill should you resist." The loud voice carried easily in the small space. My mate covered her face with her hands for a moment, upset.

I wanted to kill each and every one of them for that alone.

"Get out of my way. Now."

I knew that voice.

No. Gods, no.

Doctor Helion, I.C. Commander and evil fucking bastard walked through the door. "I told you, Kovo, a mate changes nothing." He glanced to the corner at Adrian and gave her a slight bow. "I am sorry, Adrian Davis. I truly am, but this was not meant to be."

My beast roared, leaping forward to kill the fucker and everyone with him.

Helion lifted a very large weapon from his side and pointed it at me. A heavy net flew through the air. The next instant the thick wires dug into my skin, wrapped tightly around me and sent shocks of electrical current through my body.

I dropped to the floor like a rock, the continuous current making my body twitch, my back arch in agony.

I heard Adrian scream.

My beast roared.

"Put him down. I don't want to listen to that." Helion gave the order and a flood of darts hit my back, the same sedative they'd used last time flooded my system.

I searched for Adrian. Tears streaked her face as two warlords gently attempted to convince her to leave the room.

She yanked her arm from their hold. "Don't touch me! Don't you fucking touch me."

Free of her escort, she dropped to her knees next to me and reached out with one hand.

"Do not touch him, Ms. Davis. The current in that net would likely cause your heart to fail." Doctor Helion's voice was cold, completely devoid of emotion.

Fucking icy bastard.

Her hand, mere inches from my face, balled into a fist as she looked at me. "I love you."

The words settled into my soul. I had told her countless times while we were here. That she was mine. That I loved her. Would kill for her. Die for her.

She had not said the words to me. Until now.

What a fucking tragedy this was turning out to be. And there was nothing I could do. I had failed her. Failed in every possible way.

"Get her out of here. She doesn't need to see this."

I fought to stay awake. I fought for her.

I failed.

The last thing I saw was my mate kicking, screaming and fighting as a warlord lifted her with one arm around her waist and carried her out of the room.

As I faded away, Helion knelt down next to my head. "I'm sorry, my friend. This is how it has to be."

11

Adrian

*H*elion's guards escorted me to Max's mansion, dropped me on the proverbial doorstep and left without a word.

Jerks.

When my mother saw me, she gave a soft cry, rushed forward and wrapped me in her arms.

I broke down. I'd held it together until that moment, but something about having Mom there to *'make things all better'* broke the dam I'd been using to hold in my emotions.

"That asshole! He betrayed us. He was supposed to arrange transport for us but he showed up with a small army and shot this net thing over Kovo so he couldn't fight. Then I couldn't even touch him because it would give me a heart attack and they dragged him out of there like a sack of potatoes. It was terrible. I hate him. I *hate him*."

I had never hated another person in my life, always thought hate was nothing more than a big waste of energy. I mean, why give so much of your time, energy, and emotion to someone who doesn't matter to you? Right?

But right now, I fucking *hated* that Prillon.

"I want to kill him, Mom. I want to take one of those blasters and kill him. Dead. So dead." The entire ride here I had used visions of Helion's head exploding at the end of my space gun to shove back what I didn't want to see in my head. Kovo on the ground, muscles in spasm, his entire body arched in pain as the electrical current from that net surged through him like a lightning strike. Not only logic told me Kovo was in pain, I'd sensed it through this new link I had to him. So much pain, and all he wanted, all beast wanted, was to protect me.

Helion. No way I was going back to Earth now. I was going to find a way to take down the Prillon. Kill him. Something. He needed to die. He was evil. Pure and simple. Evil with a capital E.

All out of fury, I hugged my mom and sobbed into her shoulder. "I love him. I can't do this. I can't lose him like this. I just can't."

Max came over, now that I had stopped ranting, and wrapped both of us up in his huge arms.

"What are we going to do?" Mom asked, looking up at her mate.

"I do not know, but we must hurry."

The worried tone of his voice was one I rarely heard. "Why? What's wrong? What's happening?"

He sighed as Stefani came into the room. "Group hug? I'm in!"

Mom and I opened our arms for Stefani to join the circle. This was how we had always been, tougher together. We'd added Max to this family circle and he had made us even stronger. Stef looked at me.

"Why do you look like you've been crying for a week? Shouldn't you still be in the honeymoon phase?"

"They surrounded the little apartment and took Kovo back to jail."

"What?" She looked from Mom to Max for confirmation. "But that wasn't part of the plan."

"I know."

"My ladies. My loves. We must gather our things and go. Now."

"Go where?" Mom asked.

"They just announced Kovo's capture on the news. He is to be executed within the hour."

***

Atlan Prison, Execution Wing

"Get out of my way. I'm going in there." I shoved at the

hulking form of a guard with no effect. He didn't even need to adjust his balance.

Shit. I needed to start working out.

Screw that. I needed one of those space guns.

I felt Max's presence come up behind me. "Open the door, warlord."

He shook his head. "No females allowed in the execution chamber, sir. I am sorry."

"She is his mate."

I held up my wrists to put the mating cuffs on display. I hadn't been able to sense Kovo through our link, but he had to be okay. He had to. I couldn't think anything else or I wouldn't be able to get through this.

The guard looked from my wrists to Max. "Are you sure about this, sir? It is no place for a lady, especially a mate."

"I am sure. Open the door. That is an order."

The guard looked defeated. Max was some big deal here, on a war council. Like a five star general back home. This guard was going to open the freaking door or I would scratch his eyes out like a cat.

More like a tiny kitten attacking a bear.

Whatever. This kitten was pissed off.

The guard opened the door to reveal a long, sterile corridor. It felt like a high-tech hospital, but there were no rooms. No windows to look into. No doors. I ran as quickly as I could, the boots Kovo made for me making almost no sound when they hit the floor.

Max walked behind me. My mom and Stef had to

wait in another area of the prison. The only reason I was allowed to be there was because I was Kovo's mate. I also had Max with me to look big and scary and boss people around.

Normally, it was almost impossible to guess what my mom's mate was thinking at any given moment. He had an excellent poker face. But he'd been in that room with Helion and Warden Egara on the comms. They'd worked out the plan to save Kovo together. Get him out of prison, hide him for a few days until the hunt cooled, then transport him to Warden Egara on Earth where she would use her contact with an FBI or CIA friend of hers, some woman she knew, to get Kovo a new identity. After that, Kovo and I would live happily-ever-after.

That was the plan.

Other warlords were living on Earth now. Technically, she would be in trouble if anyone ever found out she had helped us that way, on Earth or in the Coalition. I had learned this past week that Warden Egara had no problems breaking the rules if she thought it was the right thing to do.

Me and Kovo together? That was right.

Not this.

The corridor opened up onto a circular balcony that wrapped around more than half of the room situated below. An observation deck. Below us, Kovo was strapped to what looked like a hospital bed. He looked like he was dead already.

I panicked. Couldn't breathe. "Oh, god. We're too late."

Max placed a warm hand on my shoulder. "No. Look there." He pointed to a screen on the side of the wall below that I hadn't noticed before. "Those are his vitals. He is sedated, but still alive."

My knees wobbled and I hung onto the chest high wall—waist high on Max—so I wouldn't fall. I leaned over as best I could to inspect the rest of the room. Doctor Helion stood with his arms crossed at the head of Max's bed. He looked like the demon he was.

I would hunt him down. I would find out how much one of those Elite Hunters cost and hire one to find him and kill him. He'd masterfully orchestrated Reji's fake death. Great. Go, team. But to do it, he'd convinced Kovo to take the fall. For that, I would fucking hire all of the Elite Hunters. Every. Single. One. They would have to bring me Helion's head. I wanted proof.

One level below us there was a smaller group of balconies, more like the box seats at a theater. Each one of them was full of what I assumed was the Atlan version of the media. They all jostled for position, peeking around one another to get a better look at the infamous warlord who had betrayed his people and murdered his own brother.

It was unheard of in a male who did not have mating fever.

Then again, they all believed he had been an out of control psycho when he'd supposedly killed his brother.

Kovo told me he'd acted like a raging beast in order to fool them.

Well, he'd done a damn fine job. Idiot.

I wanted to scream the truth at them but knew I could not. Revealing the truth would invalidate Kovo's sacrifice. It would mean his baby brother's death.

I knew about siblings. I had Stef. If anyone messed with her I would stop at nothing to make sure she was okay. Kovo loved his brother. I could not betray his trust. I could not be the reason Reji died—for real this time.

Max squeezed my shoulder. "I'm going down there to speak with Helion. See what I can do."

"Okay."

"You must remain here, do you understand? If you go anywhere else, you will be hauled out of here kicking and screaming. I won't' be able to do anything to get you back in."

"I know. You told me."

"I would see you happy, daughter. Let us hope Helion listens to reason."

I scoffed. "He won't."

"Then perhaps he will listen to threats."

Shocked at Max's words, I looked up at him. "You're going to threaten him?"

Max's eyes narrowed. "If he hurts you, I am going to kill him. He is Prillon. He is a spy. He has no protection on Atlan but what we choose to give him."

I nodded. Max walked away as I contemplated his words.

Helion at the mercy of Max and the war council?

Hope flared back to life in my heart. Surely, even Helion would not want to anger the entire Atlan war council. Lots of badass, experienced warlords like Max who were not intimidated by his size or his job. If Helion wasn't at least cautious, he was an idiot.

I turned to find the Prillon looking right at me.

Our gazes locked. All I saw behind his alien eyes was ice cold calculation.

Fucking bastard. He was going to go through with this execution. He was going to sacrifice Kovo to save Reji and whatever stupid mission Reji had been sent on.

No!

I ran in the direction Max had gone a few minutes earlier. There had to be an entrance down there. I didn't care how small I was. There had to be something I could do. Pull tubes out of a wall, disconnect an I.V.—if they even used those. *Something.*

Strangle that Prillon with my bare hands. If he hurt me, Max would kill him. I was confident in that. Having an Atlan for a stepfather was turning out to be pretty handy.

I hoped.

A strange bell sounded through the corridor and I picked up my pace. I realized I was three floors above Kovo.

I ran until I found an elevator. I pushed the button, or what I thought was the button.

Nothing happened. No lights. No ding. No sound of a car moving up and down in the elevator shaft.

Shit. Was this an elevator? I didn't actually know.

Frantic now, I raced past it to where a series of doors lined the hall. I tried each one. All of them were locked.

"Shit." I kicked the last door I'd tried with my boot. "Shit. Shit. Shit." I should have insisted on going with Max when he left. Now I was trapped up here. None of the scanners worked to open the doors, at least not with my handprint. The elevator wasn't an elevator. Even if it were, I couldn't get it to work.

My eyes burned as I raced back the way I had come. Maybe there were doors on the *other* side, where we'd come in.

Why hadn't I thought of that before?

Because that will take you back down that empty walkway with no doors, back to the guard who didn't want to let you in here at all.

God. No. Just no.

I reached the overlook where I'd stood a few minutes earlier. This time I was drenched in sweat, my heart pounded, my eyes burned. Adrenaline had to be flooding my system because all I wanted to do was run, screaming, into the execution room and drag Kovo out of there.

Except he weighed at least three times what I did. I'd learned the last few days that there was no moving a beast who did not wish to be moved. Nor one that was sleeping. I'd tried nudging him over when he hogged the little bed. No luck. Which was fine. I'd ended up crawling on top of him and sleeping on his chest. No regrets on that score.

I leaned over the wall to see what was going on. Not much had changed except Helion was reading a list of Kovo's crimes to the witnesses on the floor below me. The spectators in the theater boxes.

Who would want to be here for this kind of thing?

Several of them were holding recording devices of some kind. No doubt to broadcast on their version of news.

Reporters. That's who was here. Two military looking Atlans were in the box closest to Kovo. The rest were filled with spectators who leaned over eagerly, some obviously excited about watching my mate die.

Shit.

I had to figure out a way to get down there. I had to.

Desperate for a way to reach Kovo, I leaned over farther than I had before, looking for anything I could hold onto to crawl down.

There was nothing like a fireman's pole for me to slide down. There were, however, a series of decorative metal links that looked like they helped hold up the walls as well as added decoration. Because, of course, you wanted the murder pit to look nice.

I jumped up and braced my hips on the wall's ledge. It was curved, so it wasn't as painful as I had anticipated. Leaning over as far as I dared, I removed the long scarf-like wrap Kovo had made for me and tied one end as tightly as I could around one of the metal links. The fabric was strong enough to hold me. It was only about nine feet long, but that was nine feet closer to the ground. If I hung from the very end with my arms over my head, the remaining fall would be...ten feet? Eight? It was hard to tell from here.

I yanked on the knot to test it. It held. I looked down into the center of the chamber again.

Where was Max? Why wasn't he in there raising hell?

And what was Helion...

"No!" I screamed. Helion looked up just as I swung my legs out over the ledge and slid down my wrap, clinging desperately to the end. My feet swung in the air. Instinctively I kicked for balance, but it did not help.

I was slipping.

I glanced down and wanted to cry. This place was a lot bigger than it looked. I had a solid twenty foot drop beneath me.

"No, female!" Doctor Helion yelled at me. I ignored him. He was the enemy.

The others looked up as well, the medial staff I had not been able to see from up above. Two Atlans stood behind some sort of control stations.

The large monitor I'd seen from above was directly across from me, at eye level.

Kovo's heartbeat was a flat line.

I broke.

My hands slipped from the rope and I plummeted to the ground. My ankle twisted, pain shooting up my leg, intensified until I felt my bones crack.

Broken leg? I didn't care.

I'd made it. I was here.

I crawled across the floor and dragged myself up the side of Kovo's bed, standing on the leg that still worked. I touched his face. Already his body was going cold. "I'm here, Kovo. I'm here."

I collapsed over his chest, the broad, warm chest I'd slept on just a few hours earlier. And heard nothing. No heartbeat. No breathing. Sobs churned in my chest, rising from my broken heart to choke me.

He was gone. They'd already done it. They'd killed him.

I lifted my head to find Helion. I was going to rip his throat out with my teeth.

There. Just a few steps away.

Leaving Kovo, I lunged for him.

Agony sliced me in half and I collapsed to the floor as my broken leg gave out.

Helion looked me right in the eye. "It had to be done."

"No! There was another way. You didn't have to do this!" I sobbed, my heart shattered into a million pieces.

He turned away from me and nodded at someone guarding the door I'd never been able to reach. The entrance appeared, as did two large Atlans dragging Max between them. They'd caught him in the same kind of net they'd used on Kovo.

My scream was primal rage. I pushed past the physical pain. Fear. I had Elite Hunter blood in my veins. A broken leg would not stop me, not when Helion was so fucking close.

I rose, standing on the broken leg. The pain only fueled my rage. "I'm going to kill you."

Helion sighed as if I were a bothersome child and gave a slight nod to someone I could not see.

Huge, powerful arms wrapped around me from behind. Whoever had ahold of me picked me up and carried me like I weighed no more than a stuffed animal. "Medical, sir?" The voice behind me asked.

"Yes. Get them both to medical." He pointed at Max as he spoke. "And make sure she gets that leg treated."

"Yes, sir."

I kicked. I cried. I screamed. I scratched the warlord's arms. If I'd had a way to reach him, I would have sunk my teeth into him as well.

Nothing worked. He carried me away. Away from Kovo. Away from Helion. Away from my dead mate."

12

Adrian

The warlord carried me to their medical treatment room. The place wasn't large, but reminded me of the hospital morgues I saw on T.V. shows. All metal, cold and sterile.

The doctor who walked toward me with one of those glowing magic wands was not Helion, thank god. I'm pretty sure I would have tried to find something in here to stab him.

Did they still use scalpels in space?

Or knives?

Hell, I'd take a nice metal hanger at this point.

"Hello." The doctor's voice was soothing and calm. And female. Which let me breathe a bit easier. I was done with men right now. Males. Of every species.

When I didn't say anything, just sat there with tears leaking from my eyes to run down my face, she indicated my leg. "May I? I need to take a look at that."

"Fine." It didn't hurt anymore, not like it had before. I was pretty sure I was in shock or something, but I didn't really care. Kovo was dead. There was nothing I could do about it. I loved him and he was gone. "Do you know how much it costs to hire an Elite Hunter to kill someone?"

The doctor, who had been gently lifting my legs up onto the examination table, stopped cold and looked at me from the corner of her eye. "No. I'm sorry. I do not have that information."

"Figures. Thought I'd ask."

The Atlan woman, female, had mating cuffs on. They were not as elaborate as my mother's, but they were gorgeous. Sparkling silver over dark pewter. The tones were in three dimensional patterns that made it appear as if she wore flowing water on her wrists.

"Your mating cuffs are beautiful."

"Thank you." She worked at cutting my pants from the hem up so she could get to my leg. She wasn't having much luck. "You are wearing battle armor."

"I am?" Of course I was. Kovo would have made sure I was as protected as he could make me.

"Yes. Very high quality. Where did you get this? It is not standard issue, not the correct color."

I looked at the clothes. They weren't jeweled or inscribed with a family crest or motto. They were plain.

Simple. Like love. Love was simple. You either did, or you didn't. "My mate made it for me."

"You were Kovo's mate?"

"Yes." I wanted to scream at her that I was *still* Kovo's mate, but she had referred to him in the past tense. As in dead. Guess I wasn't his anymore. He was dead, which meant he definitely wasn't mine.

She retrieved a different gadget and placed it over the armor covering my leg. A zipper-like portion appeared out of nowhere. The doctor unzipped it and rolled it up my leg. "Battle armor is made for quick and easy removal."

I had clothes with magic zippers. I should be excited, or at least curious.

I was numb.

She scanned me with her tools and nodded her head as if pleased. "You fractured both bones in this leg, but the armor prevented it from being worse. I believe the ReGen wand will repair the damage. However, if you prefer, I can place you in a ReGen pod for a few hours."

I shrugged. Did. Not. Care. Kovo was gone.

She worked on my leg, could have been five minutes or five hours. I had no sense of the passing of time. I wasn't paying attention to much of anything until I heard an all too familiar voice.

"Where is she?"

Helion.

The doc was running her scans again, I assumed to make sure the healing was done. I swung my legs over the bed and stood, looking for a weapon. Anything I could use to attack him. Hurt him.

Hurt him like I was hurting.

He glanced up at that moment. Our gazes locked and it was as if he were reading my mind.

"Where is Max?" I asked.

"He is fine. He was taken to another area and released from the net. Nothing was injured but his pride."

"Nothing but his pride?" I took another step toward him. "You." I was so out of sorts I literally couldn't form words with my mouth and tongue. "You."

"I am deeply sorry, my lady. It was never my intention to see you involved in any of this."

"You killed him!"

He looked over my head at the doctor behind me. "Do you have a light sedative, perhaps? I will deliver her safely home."

"Don't you dare. You are a monster! You know that?" Something weird felt like it was shot into my back. Not a needle. Just kind of flowing through my skin. I took a step. Two. I swayed on my feet and it was the Prillon I hated most in the entire universe who caught me. "Don't touch me," I slurred.

He ignored me and picked me up, cradled me in his arms like a sleeping three-year-old who needed to be carried to bed. "Thank you, Doctor."

"Of course."

"Her leg?"

"Healed. She might be sore for a few days. And before

you ask, I scanned her for other injuries. Other than elevated adrenaline and heart rate, she is physically well."

"Excellent. I will inform her family."

Helion turned and carried me out of the medical area. I was loopy, but not asleep. "Where are you taking me?" Again with the slurring. What was in that drug?

"Home."

Home? I wanted to cry. Earth wasn't home. Atlan wasn't home. Kovo was home, and he was dead. "I hate you."

"I am aware."

"No, you don't get it. I *hate* you. I want to claw your eyes out."

"Why do you not?"

I thought about that and spoke truthfully. Whatever that doctor had given me wasn't just a sedative, more like a truth serum. "My arms feel too heavy. I can't lift them."

The jerk actually chuckled. "Do you love Kovo, Adrian?"

"I won't tell you anything about him. You shouldn't even be speaking his name."

"Do you love him? It is a simple question."

"I don't trust you."

"Then you are wise as well as beautiful."

"You're strange."

"Do you love him? Would you die for him? Stay with him forever? Bare his children? Care for him if he were ill? Accept and love his beast as much as you claim to love him?"

"Yes."

"Which question are you answering?"

"All of them." I thought this super-spy, doctor, mega-asshole was supposed to be smart. "You're stupid for a doctor. I thought doctors had to be smart."

"No one has insulted me to my face for years."

"A tragedy. You might not be such an ass if they had."

He laughed this time, a full-throated laugh that completely transformed him from a demon to something different. Something not quite as scary. I still hated him, but sustaining the emotion was more difficult.

Or maybe that was just the drugs.

"Here we are." Two Prillon guards stood outside the door. They each nodded at him as the door opened and Helion carried me inside.

I blinked to clear my vision and looked around. Nothing I saw made sense. Was this a factory of some kind? Under the prison? There were huge metal boxes, three times as tall as the Warlords next to them. They glowed from the inside like small suns. The floors were dark, bare and smooth as glass. There were no chairs, no desks, no indication of what was happening.

At the center of each giant box, someone stood. Sometimes multiple people. Some elderly, some children. Always, they looked sad.

As sad as I felt. "What is this place?"

"The crematorium."

I struggled in his arms, fought to get down. I was already better than a few moments ago, but I was still only at about half strength. Even at full strength, I didn't stand a chance against him.

"Hush, this will be over soon."

He took me to one of the large boxes—crematories—where, I realized, they burned their dead. "I don't want Kovo's ashes."

"There will be no ashes."

We waited in silence for long minutes. I didn't feel like talking, and apparently, neither did he. A bright glow emanated from the machine, the colors not like the others I'd seen. This one had a tinge of yellow but was mostly green. Kovo's name appeared across the front of the device. About a minute later, a small light came on.

Helion nodded to one of the guards I hadn't realized were following us. The Prillon stepped forward, opened what had been an invisible compartment and removed a green and gold crystal about as tall as my forearm was long. It was beautiful. Glittering when the light caught it just right.

"What is that?"

The Prillon guard walked to me slowly and held out the object. I took it with shaking hands and placed it against my chest.

"That was Kovo's request. A green and gold memorial stone that matched your eyes."

I clutched the stone tightly. Kovo's last gift to me. Numbness turned to overwhelming grief. Tears flooded my entire being and leaked from my eyes as Helion carried me toward another large door.

"Where are you taking me now?"

"Home, Adrian Davis."

I didn't argue as he placed me gently in the back of a vehicle and closed the door.

The two Prillon guards slid into the front two seats and drove away without a backward glance at Helion.

And that, I decided, would be the last time I ever had to see that asshole's face. Sure, he'd honored Kovo's last wish. He'd been somewhat kind to me. But he'd killed my mate. I didn't care about the bargain the three of them had made. Kovo, Reji and Helion. When Kovo found a mate, they should have changed the terms. Made a new agreement.

What kind of ice did that Prillon have running in his veins that he could watch a good man like Kovo die, knowing he was innocent?

Helion knew the truth. He *knew*.

He killed my mate anyway.

The driver and his sidekick drove me back to Max's mansion in silence. Which was just fine with me. I didn't want to talk. Couldn't.

My mother was waiting on the doorstep. I ran into her arms.

She let me sob into her shoulder as the vehicle drove away. "Come inside, baby girl. Come on."

"Mom, he's dead!" I wailed.

"I know, honey, I know."

She walked, I stumbled past multiple members of the household staff. My sister ran to me when she saw me and wrapped her arm around my other shoulder. "Adrian, I'm so sorry. It's going to be okay." She looked up and all around as if she were afraid someone would overhear us.

Overhear what? Kovo was dead. I was carrying the weird version of an urn right now. This green thing was all I had left of him.

Stef looked at the strange orb. "What's that?"

"That's Kovo. It's made out of his ashes."

"Oh, shit." She leaned the side of her head against mine. "I'm so sorry."

They walked with me to the private, family wing. When we approached the door to my bedroom, they both stopped walking and let me go.

I wasn't done with them yet. I didn't want to go in there and be alone. I would do nothing but curl into a ball and sob until I couldn't get out of bed. "Aren't you coming in with me?"

Mom shook her head. "I'm sorry, dear. I will stop by later. We have some leftover guests from the the party here to discuss war strategies with Maxus. I can't. I will stop by later. Okay?" She gave me a peck on the cheek and hurried away.

Miserable, I turned to Stef, who was also backing away. "I promised Max I would do something to help him out. I can't stay either. I'm so sorry."

"What?"

Stefani turned on her heel and hightailed it down the hall.

"Wait!"

She waved over her shoulder, but kept walking.

Well shit. I was going to have to go in alone and go with the sobbing mess version of the night.

I was crying before I had the door to my room open.

I was sobbing by the time it was closed. Choking, wrenching sobs. I couldn't control it. I didn't care who heard me.

I didn't make it to the bed. I dropped to the thick carpet in front of the door and collapsed, forehead on my arms as my entire body shook with anguish.

He was gone.

"Do not. I cannot bear it."

Great, now I was hearing things, too?

13

Adrian

*N*ow I was hearing a dead man's voice.

The thought sent a wave of regret through me. I should have tried harder. I shouldn't have trusted Helion and his stupid plan. I shouldn't have gone up to that top floor with Max and been trapped up there, unable to stop them from killing...

From murdering...

"Adrian, my love. Stop at once."

I wailed like a baby, the sobbing worse. "Kovo."

Strong hands wrapped around my waist and lifted me off the floor. Before I could blink, I was pressed snuggly against a warm chest, cradled. Kovo's scent filled my head and I couldn't understand what was happening. I closed my eyes at once, not wanting to lose this feeling, deathly afraid if I opened them, the experience would fade away like my best dreams always did in the morning.

The nightmares, however, stuck like super-glue.

Was I hallucinating? Was I so out of my mind that I was seeing things? Did that drug Helion told the doctor to give me send me on some weird acid trip? Was this my Everian blood making me have visions of him?

"I am here. Love, please. Stop. You must stop."

"You're dead."

"I am holding you."

"I watched you die."

"No. You watched me be sedated while our I.C. operative placed faulty data into the system. That was not my heartbeat that stopped. Adrian, my love, listen to me. Please. I cannot bear to see you this way.

Faulty data?

"What are you talking about? You aren't even real."

He lifted my hand and held it on his cheek. "We sent the life sign data to the prison system ourselves so no one would be suspicious. No one can ever know what we did today."

"What?" I finally opened my eyes to find his big, gorgeous face hovering, looking deeply worried.

"I am here. Helion and I made a bargain once more."

"What was the deal?" Hope blossomed in my chest. Could this be happening?

"Like with Reji, he arranged to fake my death."

"And? What did he want?"

"A clean conscience, I believe. He said he had enough blood on his hands already."

No doubt about that. Asshole. Asshole. Asshole. "I want to claw his eyes out."

Kovo, my mate, smiled at me. "I can never return to Atlan again, nor any Coalition planet which the I.C. monitors."

My lungs were getting hot. I was breathing too fast. Nothing made sense. "So where are you supposed to go?" Was he going to leave me again? Go to some distant galaxy? Run away and hide?

"I'm going home with you, to Earth."

"They don't monitor us?"

"No. Not like they do the more advanced planets. On Earth, I can melt into the population and get very, very lost."

I sat up a bit straighter and looked my mate in the eyes. "Are you telling me that you faked your death and didn't tell me?" I was going to kill him. And Helion. And Warden Egara. "Did my family know?"

He shook his head. "Only Max. I needed him to make sure you didn't do anything foolish." He placed a hand on my leg and moved it around as if checking my recent injury.

"Like jump from two stories up and break my leg?"

"Exactly like that. What were you thinking? You could have broken your neck."

"I wasn't thinking. I had to get to you. I had to save you." I cried. Laughed. Cried some more.

"You already did. My mating fever was severe. I would not have lasted even a few more weeks. You found me, you claimed me, and you accepted my beast. That is what saved me. My bargain with Helion would not have been possible if I had not already been mated to you."

"Does this mean I can't hate him anymore? I was really getting good at it." I sniffed, not quite ready to let that one go.

He chuckled. "Many people have that particular talent."

I wiggled out of his arms and stood between his legs. I wrapped my arms around his neck and breathed him in. "Why didn't you tell me?" This was the question that hurt the most. He knew I was going to suffer, and he had done it anyway.

"You saw the news people, those that chase gossip. Your reaction had to be real. Authentic. I am sorry my love, but I could not tell you." He gave a command and the normally bare wall next to us transformed into a giant television screen. And there was Kovo's face, followed by an exciting retelling of today's events. When they got to me, to my scream, my jump from above, the way I lunged at Helion, there was no doubt it was real.

I had to look away. "Turn it off."

The screen went blank immediately and I had to spend long minutes calming down again. Watching it, seeing it brought up every memory and emotion. The pain. Anguish. Despair.

"I never want to see that again."

"Then you never shall. Please, love, tell me you can forgive me. I had to protect you and my brother. I could not fail. If even one of my enemies, or one I.C. officer suspected your reaction was false, thought, even for a moment, that I might be alive? You would be in danger. Reji would be in danger. I could not allow that."

"So you hurt me."

"Forgive me. I had no choice."

I sighed. His logic was infallible. I was a terrible actress and an even worse liar. There was no way I could have pulled that off if I knew it was all part of Helion's master plan. "I forgive you."

He crushed me to him, his hand stroking my back. "Mate, I will never hurt you again."

"I forgive you, on one condition."

"Anything."

"You are never, ever to make another deal with that Prillon, *ever* again."

Kovo's laughter died off and I looked up into his dark eyes. He was mine. I did not enjoy feeling what I did today, but I was also thankful. Warlord Kovo of Atlan, like his brother Reji, was officially dead now. No one would come looking for him. No one would doubt the execution broadcast live for the entire planet. A sense of joy, contentment, hope, and gratitude blossomed inside me. Kovo was alive. Safe.

And no mated female listening to my screams would doubt my reactions. They were too raw, too filled with anger and pain.

"I don't want to talk about it anymore." I leaned forward and pressed my lips to his.

Our kiss was tender and slow. Gentle.

Kovo pulled away. "I can taste tears on your lips."

I shrugged. "I did a lot of crying today."

"I cannot endure your tears." He picked me up and walked to the adjoining bathroom suite where he set me on my feet. He stripped me slowly, kissing each part of me as it was revealed. By the time he'd removed my boots, I had to hang on to his shoulder so I wouldn't tip over.

"Why am I naked and you are not?"

He grinned. "Because your body is far more beautiful than mine."

I kissed him for that, even though he was one hundred percent, totally and completely wrong. I wouldn't tell Kovo. I'd tell the beast. He wouldn't argue. He would be proud that I found his body to be perfect.

I stepped into the showering unit and started the water, getting it warm but not too hot. I had no intention of getting out any time soon. I lifted my face to the spray and washed away the remnants of my tears. I didn't want to taste them. I wanted to start over. Right now. Just me...and him.

A large body pressed into me from behind. His palms came up under my arms to cup my breasts. "You do realize this is a home owned by a warlord?"

"Of course."

He turned me to face him, lifted me in his arms and

placed my bottom on a small ledge I had failed to notice before. "What?" I looked around, stunned by how easily I remained in place. Kovo grabbed my arms, lifted them over my head and used something in the wall to hold me in place. I looked at him to find his cock was right *there*. Hard. Long. Ready for me.

I leaned forward as far as I could and took the tip— that's all that would fit—into my mouth. He shuddered, then groaned. Pulled himself away.

"No. Not yet."

I looked up into his eyes. "Why not?"

"The beast is hungry." I laughed as he changed, the beast standing before me seconds later.

"Hello there."

"Mine."

He was definitely a one word kind of guy. I didn't argue when he dropped to his knees and used his mouth on me, sucked on my clit, fucked me with his tongue.

I was so fragile, so shattered from the day that my orgasm hit me like a bolt of lightning, burning through me. I had nothing left that was strong enough to temper it. Draw it out. Deny it control.

He filled me before I'd recovered, the slow thrust of his huge cock making me come again.

"Mine."

"Fuck, yes."

***

Kovo

I allowed the beast to take her first. His rage at what I had been forced to put our mate through would last a long, long time.

Only the taste of her sweet pussy would calm him. Her cries of pleasure. He was obsessed. He *needed* her. His need was primitive, without reason or control. He simply needed her or he lost control.

Enough. I told him.

Mine.

Mine, too.

I forced him back inside me while our cock was buried deep inside her body, while our lips tasted her skin. I thrust slowly just to hear her moan. Beg.

We both wanted her to beg.

"Please. Faster. I need you," she begged.

I stilled. Tried to think around the tight pussy squeezing my hard length, the scent of her rising with every droplet of steam in the shower.

"How did you know?" Somehow, I'd felt her in my mind the same way I felt the beast. Her presence was light as a butterfly's wing. Feminine. Very different from the primal creature I'd lived with my entire life.

"He's not that bad." She laughed at me, using her inner muscles to clamp down on my cock like a vice. "I kinda like him."

I groaned. "He very much likes you."

"I don't know. I'm not sure I believe that."

Within, the beast roared, eager to get to our female. To taste her again. To fuck her. Make her scream and do it all over again. "You are playing with fire, love."

Her eyes drew me and I could not look away. "I'm playing with my mate."

"Forever? On Earth?"

She smiled. "Anywhere."

A SPECIAL THANK YOU TO MY READERS...

Want more? I've got *hidden* bonus content on my web site *exclusively* for those on my mailing list.

If you are already on my email list, you don't need to do a thing! Simply scroll to the bottom of my newsletter emails and click on the *super-secret* link.

Not a member? What are you waiting for? In addition to ALL of my bonus content (great new stuff will be added regularly) you will be the first to hear about my newest release the second it hits the stores—AND you will get a free book as a special welcome gift.

Sign up now! http://freescifiromance.com

FIND YOUR INTERSTELLAR MATCH!

YOUR mate is out there. Take the test today and discover your perfect match. Are you ready for a sexy alien mate (or two)?

VOLUNTEER NOW!

interstellarbridesprogram.com

DO YOU LOVE AUDIOBOOKS?

Grace Goodwin's books are now available as
audiobooks...everywhere.

LET'S TALK!

Interested in joining my **Sci-Fi Squad**? Meet new like-minded sci-fi romance fanatics and chat with Grace! Get excerpts, cover reveals and sneak peeks before anyone else. Be part of a private Facebook group that shares pictures and fun news! Join here:

https://www.facebook.com/groups/scifisquad/

Want to talk about Grace Goodwin books with others? Join the **SPOILER ROOM** and spoil away! Your GG BFFs are waiting! (And so is Grace) Join here:

https://www.facebook.com/groups/ggspoilerroom/

GET A FREE BOOK!

JOIN MY MAILING LIST TO BE THE FIRST TO
KNOW OF NEW RELEASES, FREE BOOKS,
SPECIAL PRICES AND OTHER AUTHOR
GIVEAWAYS.

http://freescifiromance.com

PATREON - SUBSCRIBE TODAY!

Hi there! Grace Goodwin here. I am SO excited to invite you into my intense, crazy, sexy, romantic, imagination and the worlds born as a result. From Battlegroup Karter to The Colony and on behalf of the entire Coalition Fleet of Planets, I welcome you! Visit my Patreon page for cut scenes, character interviews, short stories, writing tips and insider information on upcoming books as well as the opportunity to receive NEW RELEASE BOOKS before anyone else! See you there! ~ Grace

Grace's PATREON: https://www.patreon.com/gracegoodwin

ALSO BY GRACE GOODWIN

Surprise Mates

Rogue Enforcer

Interstellar Brides® Program Boxed Set - Books 6-8

Interstellar Brides® Program Boxed Set - Books 9-12

Interstellar Brides® Program Boxed Set - Books 13-16

Interstellar Brides® Program Boxed Set - Books 17-20

Interstellar Brides® Program: The Colony

Surrender to the Cyborgs

Mated to the Cyborgs

Cyborg Seduction

Her Cyborg Beast

Cyborg Fever

Rogue Cyborg

Cyborg's Secret Baby

Her Cyborg Warriors

Claimed by the Cyborgs

The Colony Boxed Set 1

The Colony Boxed Set 2

The Colony Boxed Set 3

Interstellar Brides® Program: The Virgins

The Alien's Mate

His Virgin Mate

Claiming His Virgin

His Virgin Bride

His Virgin Princess

The Virgins - Complete Boxed Set

Interstellar Brides® Program: Ascension Saga

Ascension Saga, book 1

Ascension Saga, book 2

Ascension Saga, book 3

Trinity: Ascension Saga - Volume 1

Ascension Saga, book 4

Ascension Saga, book 5

Ascension Saga, book 6

Faith: Ascension Saga - Volume 2

Ascension Saga, book 7

Ascension Saga, book 8

Ascension Saga, book 9

Destiny: Ascension Saga - Volume 3

Interstellar Brides® Program: The Beasts

Bachelor Beast

Maid for the Beast

Beauty and the Beast

The Beasts Boxed Set

Big Bad Beast

Beast Charming

Bargain with a Beast

Starfighter Training Academy

The First Starfighter

Starfighter Command

Elite Starfighter

Starfighter Training Academy Boxed Set

Other Books

Dragon Chains

Their Conquered Bride

Wild Wolf Claiming: A Howl's Romance

ABOUT GRACE

Grace Goodwin is a USA Today and international bestselling author of Sci-Fi and Paranormal romance with over a million books sold. Grace's titles are available worldwide on all retailers, in multiple languages, and in ebook, print, audio and other reading App formats.

Grace is a full-time writer whose earliest movie memories are of Luke Skywalker, Han Solo, and real, working light sabers. (Still waiting for Santa to come through on that one.) Now Grace writes sexy-as-hell sci-fi romance six days a week. In her spare time, she reads, watches campy sci-fi and enjoys spending time with family and friends. No matter where she is, there is always a part of her dreaming up new worlds and exciting characters for her next book.

Grace loves to chat with readers and can frequently be found lurking in her Facebook groups. Interested in joining her **Sci-Fi Squad**? Meet new like-minded sci-fi romance fanatics and chat with Grace! Get excerpts, cover reveals and sneak peeks before anyone else. Join here: https://www.facebook.com/groups/scifisquad/

Want to talk about Grace Goodwin books with others? Join the **SPOILER ROOM** and spoil away! Your GG BFFs are waiting! (And so is Grace) Join here:

https://www.facebook.com/groups/ggspoilerroom/